Mascara

Mascara

A Novel

ARIEL DORFMAN

SEVEN STORIES PRESS

New York • London • Toronto • Melbourne

Seven Stories Press
140 Watts Street
New York, NY 10013
www.sevenstories.com

IN CANADA
Publishers Group Canada, 250A Carlton Street, Toronto, ON M5A 2L1

IN THE UK
Turnaround Publisher Services Ltd., Unit 3, Olympia Trading
Estate, Coburg Road, Wood Green, London N22 6TZ

IN AUSTRALIA
Palgrave Macmillan, 627 Chapel Street, South Yarra VIC 3141

LIBRARY OF CONGRESS CATALOGING-IN-PUBLICATION DATA
Dorfman, Ariel.
  Mascara : a novel / Ariel Dorfman.— 1st pbk. ed.
    p. cm.
  ISBN 1-58322-641-9 (pbk. : alk. paper)
  1. Women—Fiction. 2. Girls—Crimes against—Fiction. 3. Identity
(Psychology)—Fiction. 4. Plastic surgeons—Fiction. 5. Authoritarianism—
Fiction. 6. Age (Psychology)—Fiction. 7. Revenge—Fiction. I. Title.
PR9309.9.D67M37 2004
863'.64—dc22
                              2004012308

College professors may order examination copies of
Seven Stories Press titles for a free six-month trial period.
To order, visit www.sevenstories.com/textbook/ or
fax on school letterhead to 212.226.1411.

Book design by India Amos
Cover design by POLLEN/Stewart Cauley

Printed in Canada
9 8 7 6 5 4 3 2 1

This book is for María Angélica

Acknowledgments

In this novel of deception and betrayal, the reader will be hard pressed to find human beings who show a hint of loyalty to one another. It is particularly gratifying, therefore, to acknowledge in real living people a quality that the characters, in *Mascara* at least, do not possess.

The unflagging faithfulness which Nan Graham, my editor, has shown toward me, my family and my work has sustained us all during the harrowing times when I was writing this novel. Not to mention her intelligence and stubborn insistence on making my writing as clear and direct as possible. Nor could the novel have been finished without the encouragement, almost day by day, of my agent, Andrew Wylie, whose enthusiasm for this book, fortunately, was contagious.

Mascara

FIRST

So we're finally going to meet, Doctor. Face to face, so to speak. Two o'clock this afternoon in your consulting room. Your nurse just confirmed our appointment. After lunch, that is, she said to me. As if I had any interest in lunching with you, Doctor.

Yes, Doctor, I'm talking to you, Mavirelli, or whatever your name is. It's true that I'm speaking softly and just as true that you're not even present yet. A pity your ears are less nimble and far-reaching than your fingers. You could prepare yourself for what I'm going to propose today at two. Instead of assuming that I'll deliver my unconditional surrender.

Not a chance, Doctor. If you really knew me, your deceiving hands wouldn't touch upon such a bizarre idea. But we won't have time to further our acquaintance. So this story that I'll tell to the face of yours that's in my head will have to do. If many years ago I had taken the precaution to stuff your features inside my camera, if I had snapped a photograph of you, things would be different now. You'd be the one asking me for an appointment.

Of course you won't receive me at two o'clock sharp. You'll give yourself time to look at me, at both of us, through a half-open door, some one-way mirror. You'll tell yourself you know everything about me that there is to know.

But you know nothing of my eyes, Doctor. Your spies cannot have informed you of them. They would have had to be present five days ago when I exercised my own right to look, when I gave myself the time to calmly contemplate, through the slit in the curtains of my window, that woman who called herself Patricia. What

better way of beginning to explain to you who I am, what I want?
Of course, it makes no difference where one begins to tell a story:
we always reach the same ending, don't we?

As for so-called Patricia, nobody was going to open the door
to her. At least I wasn't, and there was nobody else at home. So I
took my time examining her bit by bit. That's right, as if she were
undressing. That's why zoos are such a pleasure, Doctor; they were
when I was a kid. That terrorized animal—she was far more frightened than the first time she came to my door, it was spilling out of
her, far more—that animal which called itself, for now, Patricia
couldn't guess that someone was giving her the once over.

She's going to ring the buzzer, I thought. A first, energetic sounding; then a couple of vacant moments; after that a timid chirp of
a buzz that doesn't want to show impatience, a longer period in
which she won't know what to do, if she should stay or leave, one
last attempt, the long wait before she withdraws. A camera would
have captured for later a sequence of Patricias, with one face after
the other decomposing, fear rising in her like water that can't be
flushed away. Entertainment for a few minutes—maybe that Friday morning's lone offering.

But it wasn't my intention to take her picture. At least not then.
The camera's always ready and more so on a holiday; the feet, always
prepared to follow the person these eyes of mine have chosen. But
not that morning. Nor was Patricia's face steeped in a mystery
worth exploring. If she was coming back to my house again, it was
because she was still stuck with the same problem she had when
she came to see me the first time, the day before yesterday. Her
problem had two legs attached to it, and those two legs were probably somewhere nearby, out of sight around the corner, hoping for
a refuge they wouldn't get, at least here. Or so I had sworn at the
time. When the supposed Patricia would tire of ringing and these
eyes would tire of scanning her, each of us would return to our
little dilemma, I to the list I had in my hand, thanks to you, Doctor, the list of contacts who had passed themselves off as my allies
and whom I had been calling systematically on the phone, crossing them out one by one with what might almost be pronounced
satisfaction, because I was merely confirming a disloyalty I had
always anticipated, and she, she, on the other hand . . .

But that's not the way it went. Not even the corner of her mouth trembled, not even the thinness of those lips that her careful ochre-red rouge was trying to disguise, not even an eyelash. She pushed her finger into the buzzer and the initial shrillness sounded in the house and went on, like a sour lemon of a trumpet, went on here in this head of mine. These eyes measured the paleness of that pressed finger, the contrast with the calm liquid quiet of the rest of her body, the fury of the trapped bee in that finger, and they realized all of a sudden that the vixen knew for a certainty that there was someone at home and that the someone was none other than myself. Because a while ago the phone had interrupted the silence, and this mouth had muttered a hello, hello, with the idiotic hope that it would be one of those who had vowed their faithfulness to me, returning my calls, offering to find a witness against you, Doctor Maravirelli, before next Wednesday, at the preliminary hearing on our lawsuit.

On the other end of the line, they hung up.

"Son of a bitch!"

Someone had been calling periodically since the accident. I had come home directly from the police station, without even approaching—I would have to have been crazy—the hospital as they had recommended, limping from the pain, and the phone was already ringing. That same Wednesday—Christmas Eve, Marivelli, that first call. You work fast. That first empty hum on the line when I answered—and the knowledge that someone was tracking me down. Since then, over and over and over, that muffled purr and then these hands sweating for minutes on the dead receiver, unable to reconstruct the face of that enemy from the muted breath on the other end, the identity of the person—or persons?—that you have hired to destroy me, Doctor. The same shadow that, undoubtedly, during the last few days has been calling without respite each name in this address book of mine, in alphabetical order, as if he had the booklet itself to consult. Phoning to murmur rumors to each of them, perhaps threats. Until nobody wanted to answer my calls—sorry, he's not at home—scared of my voice—if you want to leave a message . . .

I should have worried, Mavirelli. It's been so many years since I have had that sort of experience, people denying me what I demand.

People who owe me everything, whom I have made into celebrities, saved from an insipid existence. I thought it would be enough to go to my office on Monday, enough to look up their files and their photos, and the traitors would crawl back on their knees to beg forgiveness. Then I would not only flourish three, four, as many as twenty witnesses in your face, Doctor Mierdavelli, I would also find out who was acting as your lackey, who was punching my number with a long finger. And in the worst of cases there was always one name you couldn't know about, one at least that wasn't in my booklet. I was in no hurry. It was a holiday, the day after Christmas, and there were no elevator boys on the job. Climb to the fourteenth floor? With this bandaged leg? Better to wait till Monday.

A mistake. Not to have rushed to my files right away. Yes, and also a mistake to have shouted son of a bitch. Daughter of a bitch would have been more accurate, or simply bitch, because the buzzer's persistence was revealing the true identity of the person who had called and hung up this morning.

But not the other times. It hadn't been her then. Patricia wasn't collaborating with you, Marvirelli, she wasn't your spy, or your informer. Probably didn't even know you. Our accident—and that's what it was, Doctor, an entirely unexpected, fortuitous collision of cars which neither of us desired—that accident had occurred precisely a couple of hours after she had come to see me that first time. Her neutrality attracted me. That's what forestalled my urge to disconnect the buzzer and let her rot there forever or until the police would come to carry her off, pseudonym and all. Down there, at my door, was one person in the world who was not in my address book and who had therefore not been poisoned by your flunky's efforts, Doctor. I rose with difficulty from my chair. One person who wasn't prejudiced against me, who might even be neutral. One person to have a little fun with. I towed my damaged leg down each step of the stairs. Patricia, exasperating as she was, was better than no one. With each painful step, I thought of another reason to open the door. Until I found myself, in fact, opening the door. A mistake.

Because once you've opened a door, Maravillo, it's almost impossible to shut it. You must know that. Once you begin to operate on a face, once you've transplanted one sliver of skin and everything else that your butcher's hands plunder underneath that skin, there is no way back to the person as she once was. Once you make that first thrust, Doctor, after that, the patient's fucked. Just the tip. The tip of the shoe, the tip of the tongue, the tip of whatever it is we have between our legs, the tip of that bitch Patricia's breasts—it's enough that someone should pierce us with the tingle, the dawn of a scalpel, and we're fucked. Who sticks it into whom, that's the only question worth answering in this world—or have you got a different question, Mirlaveri?

"I'm not deaf, you know."

"I'm in a hurry," said the woman who had called herself Patricia the last time we had spoken. "Is the man of the house in?"

Not even forty-eight hours had passed since she had asked this same face exactly the same question in the same place, not more than forty-eight hours, and she no longer remembered. To her, I was less than a speck of dust that is washed away by a tear. I didn't care. You won't recognize me, either, Doctor, when you inspect me through the split-second frame of your door. Your eyes will slip over my face as if they were made of soap, sliding through my features like rain on a darkened waterfall.

It's been happening to me since I can remember. Before I can remember. There's proof that they used to forget to give that kid his bottle. Why's that brat squealing? Suppose he's hungry? Impossible—we gave him his—and then they realized that no, they hadn't given that baby a piss of milk. These are not guesses, Doctor. I've read my own medical record. Don't get so upset, Miralevi. I've got access to the records of all the citizens of this land. Surely you understand that I would consult my own—before I shredded it so nobody could ever find me. There were the notes of some nurse at whose window I will arrive one day with my implacable camera: a bottle every ten, every twelve, every eighteen hours, huh, nurse? Do you think she works for you, now, Doctor? Is she one of the staff who was aiming the reflectors in your operating room yesterday? Will I encounter her this afternoon presiding over your waiting room—and she won't recognize me today, either? Is that what will happen?

I won't make things easy for her, for you, for anybody. Or for Patricia. She had been, without a doubt, most amply replenished

with milk on the strictest of schedules, not to mention the probably generous tits of a mother who remembered her name and the
color of her eyes. So I'll let Patricia, just like you, Doctor, this afternoon—I'll let you all figure out your mistake on your own.

She was clever, I'll admit that, and quick. Ten seconds later,
when she began to wonder if the man of the house wasn't, in fact,
standing composed right there in front of her, she took advantage
of the fact that the accident had left me in a dreadful state, to
excuse herself.

"Hey, now. What happened to you? Didn't recognize you."

That familiar hey, now, wasn't to my liking. "An accident," I
answered. "My car is worth shit." Measuring how much she needed
my help, how much false sympathy she was ready to deal me. Just
like you measure cheekbones and nostrils, Doctor.

"So why aren't you inviting me in?"

"Should I? Have you got another letter for me?"

"The dead only write one good-bye letter. You've got yours." But
she added, "Poor little thing."

There's something that still melts, still becomes tender all over,
Doctor, when a woman speaks to me softly. Even if I know it's
hypocrisy, that it was Patricia's press agent spouting the words,
that all that gentleness was cosmetic and calculated, even so . . .
That someone in this world would treat me with the semblance
of affection . . . It must happen to you all the time: being sucked
in by somebody's splendor although you are absolutely aware that,
underneath the bronzed skin, one skeleton is just about as unen-
ticing as another.

I let her in. Gave her just enough space so she would have to make
a dancer's flexible, imperfect twist to avoid this male body, so the
feminine flesh in her left breast had to brush my arm. I was able
to imagine the wave of heat further down, further inside. Patricia
emerging from the shower, how she would dry herself out, slowly
like a cat, or with the startled, nervous movements of a dog in heat.
It's something I'll never know, Doctor. I wasn't interested in knowing it. The mere idea of following her to her home, of adding her
intimacy to my collection, was—to put it frankly—distasteful.

My hand was going to shut the door behind her when she
stopped me.

"Wait," she said. "I'm not alone."

It was then, Doctor, that I saw her for the first time. Oriana. She appeared, she materialized, she came like a miracle to my threshold. Later, I realized that both of them had planned that ambush down to the last detail. As soon as Patricia was inside the house, the woman whom I still call Oriana today, because I have no better name for her, was to turn the protective corner, cross the street, enter my life. But at that moment what I felt was admiration for the way in which Patricia had managed to fool me, the way she had found to extract a full-grown woman with dark glasses out of thin air.

Those dark glasses of Oriana's. It wasn't necessary to read her eyes in order to surmise what the morning, probably the preceding week had been, the slow exhausting of possible sanctuaries, the boarding of the next bus, the act of getting off at an unknown stop, of gauging how many people were still left until they returned to this house which they had visited before, how many people would observe them still from the heights of some window without the slightest show of pity, until they had drained the list and found themselves returning dispassionately to the surname my parents gave me as their only gift—which I didn't want, anyway—when they pushed me into this world. My surname, which Patricia had already crossed off her list once two days ago. And if the door had not opened, what would they have done? Would they have stood there in front of the house, like a couple of tombstones or dead horses? Or would they return, punctual, insistent, sterile, every two days?

All of a sudden, here inside, a warning. Here inside, an unknown desire, so unrecognizable and dangerous that it felt like a slap. What I wanted was their return. Correction: I didn't want them ever to leave. Correction again: Patricia and her contact lenses could go to hell. The one I didn't want to leave was the other one, the new one, the woman who at that moment did not yet have a name.

Describe her, Doctor? Beautiful, Doctor? Let's suppose that she is. For you, for other men, it matters that you should be seen with a flashy woman, who awakens everybody else's envy. But these eyes know, and yours should as well, Doctor, of what tricks and shades the loveliness of human beings is composed. And she—well, it was as if she came from a world where nobody had ever heard of Helena

Rubinstein, where the touched-up portrait had not been invented, where the yellow gloves of surgeons such as you, Marvirelli, are forbidden. She was hiding nothing. Which did not mean that she was mere wrapping paper. An enigma, but not one of those easy enigmas you can explore through a keyhole or a concealed camera or the recording of sighs and creaks in the bed from the next room in some second-class dive.

This is not how Oriana should be described.

I won't explain it to you this afternoon. After lunch, as your nurse pointed out. And if you could listen to me right now, I wouldn't do it, either. But since you can't hear a word I'm saying, I'll take my time. Once on the radio they announced that the vice-president of some bank had committed suicide. Blew his brains out. It happens every day. To people whose face—the one they have constructed for themselves—fails them. Or to people whom even you doctors can't help by giving them a new identity. Yes, it happens every day. But in this case, he did it in front of the T V cameras, in front of a dozen photographers. They had nailed the guy in some sleazy deal: he was registering the dead as if they were alive and collecting their pensions, or he simply wasn't recording the deaths of people and was still collecting, or something of the sort, or both things. I can't remember. Conning people just like you do, Mardovelli. Swindlers. He called a press conference, and after having protested his inno- cence, he very serenely took a revolver from his attaché case and he ruined his make-up forever. Or his plastic surgery, Doctor, if he had ever passed under the lights of your clinic.

Too bad I had only one television set. The two newscasts are transmitted at the same time, so that evening I had to switch from one channel to the other, back and forth. A fruitless search. The damned journalists had reached an agreement among themselves. On the first channel, all the preliminaries, to be sure, almost the whole press conference—but no final big-bang moment. On the other, a brief news item, accompanied by a photo of the dead man before he— A fraud. A fraud. Much worse than the one that the suicide banker had perpetrated. That's how the clients of a night club must feel when the strip tease stops at the waist. Everywhere you look, censorship. At that very moment, the journalists, the personnel of each network, were enjoying the scene, enjoying their supposed horror of the scene. What right did they have to interpose themselves between the dead man and these eyes of mine? If he wanted to go public with his departure from this earth, how did they dare steal that from me?

I switched on another channel, one that wasn't transmitting anything. Like a face without skin, Doctor. I stayed there, looking at that colorless shit, that meaningless static for a long time—that's what they had transformed the man's act into, that's what they made of my eyes. To tune in to the other news made no sense. Lies, only lies. Everything a lie—except that instant which was the only truthful act that banker had ever committed in his dissembling life, his sleight-of-hand existence. A treasure that those journalists, his only spectators, because they had camouflaged it, had proven to be unworthy of. On the other hand, me—if he had decided to commit suicide in front of me . . .

And Oriana?

The brief flash of her sudden appearance was sufficient: it was as if she were exclusively made up of culminating moments, like that banker's. As if in each instant of her existence, she lived that exposed, that openly daring—but without hastening the proof, without having to kill herself, death as the only road to revelation. And there was not one inch of a bad check in her, not one internal P.R. man burning the less flattering photographs, not the hint of one vice-president inside her trying to pass the dead for the living or vice versa. The proof? I couldn't invent one scene about her in my head, I couldn't imagine, as I can with all the other women in the universe, as I just had with trumped-up Patricia, the towel with which she dries her armpit. She hasn't got—the idea zigzagged in my head like a white serpent—more than this instant, more than this face. No investigation, no file on her past, no photograph, would reveal anything different. Never in my life had I seen a transparent adult, with nothing to hide, without an artificial smile to fashion her. A person whom you—especially you, Doctor—couldn't add to or detract from. A person who never needed to retreat from other eyes. It can't be, I said to myself. It can't be.

But it could be, it was.

Patricia had taken a seat on the sofa without so much as waiting for an invitation. She crossed her legs and pulled out a pack of cigarettes. Oriana, clear as a crystal, just stood there, on one foot, scratching it with the scruff of her other shoe, as if she were expecting us to decide what we were going to play next.

"Oh, no, you don't. Not in this house—no smoking here . . . Patricia? Is that still your name?"

"Why not?" she answered brazenly. It didn't worry her that she had just admitted using an assumed name. How could she know that, merely having glimpsed her twice, if I felt like it, I could ferret out her true identity this very Monday. If I were the kind who smiles, perhaps something would have crept onto my face to let her know. But I'm not. Nobody has ever detected what I'm thinking by my lips. "Hey, Oriana, the bathroom's upstairs." That clean miracle called Oriana began to disappear up the stairway. "And don't come out till I tell you, okay?"

I don't know what shocked me more: the fact that Patricia was treating her like a defenseless little brat or the fact that a woman as mature, yes, and as splendid as Oriana would turn out to be so docile, so submissive.

I didn't bother to hide my distaste for Patricia and her tinsel-assed bossiness. She was taking over my house with the same high-handedness with which she was ordering Oriana around. Her only cordial act had been her first—that slackish, demure, almost cowardly way of knocking at my door two days before. Dissembling slut. If she had rung the bell frantically, I wouldn't have let her in, even if I had thought, as in fact I did, that it was Divine Providence herself who was sending me this tidbit the day before a Christmas that announced itself as usual, lonely and austere. No sign of Oriana that day. A pity. Because if I had caught a glance of her that Wednesday, there can be no doubt I would have told Patricia I was ready to keep her friend for a day, for a couple of days. Really a pity, because instead of going out in my car that evening, I'd have stayed at home and avoided burning that red light and colliding head on with the grand limousine, Doctor Miravelli, in which you were parading around with your lover.

But I've never been a man with luck. On that occasion, rather than extracting Oriana from her coat pocket, Patricia had taken out a letter.

"From your friend Alicia," she said.

Alicia. That's not her name, Doctor. But if I were to describe her to you, Doctor, you might remember. Not because you care about your patients, but this one—well, she was, according to the rules of fashion that you go by, a real crone. I bet you have her in your files: before and after. To persuade other hags. But that's as far as your files go, right, Doctor? You don't want to find out what becomes of your clients later on, I guess. Although you may have learned that, with the face you loaned her, she had to leave the country; you probably don't know that four years later she was dead.

The joy I felt at having received her promised dispatch was mitigated by a lash of indignation against Patricia. How dare she take this long to contact me?

"Two years," I said, not touching the damned letter with even the tip of a finger. "Couldn't you have brought it before?"

"Didn't need to," said Patricia. And before this throat of mine could accuse her of irresponsibility—what if there had been some important message?—she interrupted me as if she could read my thoughts: I didn't like that much, either—it's something I prefer to do to others. "Nothing important," she said.

"What? What's that you said?"

"Nothing important," Patricia repeated.

"And how come you know that?"

"Because I read it. You could almost say I dictated it. There're only a couple of lines and a photo."

A photo! The photo had finally come. Would it show her face before you remodeled it, before you ruined her life? Or would it be the newer version—the falsified features you dolled her up with and which, for my part, I refused to look at? Such an urgent question, and the answer could come only from Patricia's bitter tongue, from this unknown woman who, for two years, had kept my correspondence inside a drawer in her room, opening it and reading and rereading it over and over whenever it tickled her cunt. While I had thought, all this time, that Alicia had forgotten me.

It wasn't that I expected her to die with my name on her lips. But she was the one, after all, who was consuming a big bite of my existence. She was leaving me in an uncomfortable position: from now on the only confirmation of that brief week of friendship we had lived was to be found in the sterile memories dammed up inside my brain. She owed me some sort of souvenir. Something that would allow me to fool and retain the past that was departing with her. Because I did not have even one photograph of her: no one has ever been given a greater token of my affection. I won't take one, I won't accept one, I told her. But if you happen to die, send me one, so I won't be alone with my memories. Memories, I said to her, are like ham: you can slice them, devour them, digest them, shit them. A photograph: now, you can fuck a photograph forever. How romantic, she had replied sarcastically. But she cared a bit for me, Alicia, and here was the evidence. Though if she had really given a damn about me, Doctor, she wouldn't have gone ahead with the operation. She preferred the future you were offering her, Mavarillo: be someone else, alter your nose, be someone else, slip out of your skin, change your life in fifteen minutes. Confidentiality guaranteed. Never met a face I couldn't fix. She was already convinced by your commercials, Doctor. It was too late by the time we had met. A week later I dropped her off at the door to your consulting room, Doctor, with her face already bandaged. She went in. I never saw her again. She was already—that's right—someone else.

I took the photo out of the envelope. I placed it face down on the carpet. Until I was alone I didn't want to look at those eyes of hers that had already died—whether they were the ones I remembered or the more recent ones that you had sewn under her eyelids to make them beautiful. I read her letter as if someone were kicking me in the stomach.

Instead of feeling glad because Alicia had remembered me, I was beginning to hate her. What she had never done to me while she was alive, she was doing to me from her grave, manipulating me with the typical selfishness of the dead. What had attracted me to her in the first place was precisely that difference from others. That, and the fact that she was the first woman, and let me confess that she was the only one, who recognized me in my life. It may have been because she herself was so left out and on the side lines at school that she had no alternative but to take a good look at each kid, including that one kid who was on the edge of invisibility.

"Hello. Remember me?"

I was on line at a bank. The voice came from behind me, and there was no way, of course, that I could identify its owner. If I had that talent, the guy who calls me up to murmur my name over the phone and then laughs and then hangs up, that guy wouldn't stand a chance: once I'd captured his voice, I'd follow it to his hideaway, I'd squeeze his face out, drop by drop, onto celluloid as I have done with so many others in this land. But I am utterly unable to discern one tone from another. It isn't a form of deafness. It's just that I hate music. Or—to put it more mildly—I'm indifferent to music. When Alicia wanted to know why I didn't have a record or a cassette at home, my answer perhaps was not a lie: the only music I can distinguish is the kind that flickers in through the eyes. My brain doesn't seem to distinguish sounds by their vibrations, shades, tone, colors. There it is. Shades, tone, colors. Even the words I use for music are visual.

There's nothing wrong in living for the nourishment of your eyes, Doctor. It's got its compensations. To be brief: just as there are those who can easily remember melodies, I am absolutely unable to forget a face. Ever. Nobody can deceive me, Doctor, understand? Nobody can slip on a disguise that I won't see through. Nobody can alter his face, Doctor, nobody can pass under the swirl and eddy of your hands, Mardavelli, without my discovering them. But music? Not a note. A monster? Far from it. I'm merely living ahead of my time. That's where we are heading. Music is receding into the background in these times. This is not the century of sounds. I'm not denying that people still listen to songs, sure they do, but what really matters is elsewhere: the image, the lipstick, the tanning lotions. Sounds are like maids: they travel second-class.

So my indifference to the noises and jabbering that others spew forth is no deprivation. That I wasn't able even to discern the sex of the person talking to me that day in the bank was no cause for shame. On the contrary: I almost felt like inventing a smile for my face so I could inflict it upon that intruder behind me. I may not know you by your voice, but it is enough to turn toward you the deep furrow of my eyes and—if I feel like it—dredge your life from you.

I moved my head to look at whoever might own that voice. But while I was doing it, underneath the idea of a smile, I was assailed by a slight uneasiness. Because I had never heard words like those pronounced by anybody. That was my phrase, the question I had been repeating all these years, first timidly and then with despair—

remember me? Remember me?—until finally it was transformed
into, I know you don't remember me but . . . and of course they
never remembered and in my case did not even pretend to remember.
When Alicia spoke those words on the bank line that day, it had
been many years since I had fallen back onto that phrase. Many
years since I had decided I would never again ask that question or
precede that question with an explanation. I would not give the rest
of them one detail, one key to understanding who I was. It is true
that by the time I gave up asking, I already possessed other instruments to amuse me . . . I was living alone, I had already changed
my name, I was settled in at the Department of Traffic Accidents;
but above all my camera stalked the city as freely as if I had been
the Chief of Police. And Alicia had come to disturb the calm I had
acquired. She was restoring for me that obscene phrase, almost as
if someone wanted to make fun, at this late date, of what I had
once desired: to be a man like any other man, who misplaces one
person and remembers another one, who is recognized by most
people and is ignored by a few. Alicia made me feel like that man.
That is why I never followed her, I never took her photo, I never
bedded her. If she had been able to avoid the temptation of your
propaganda, Doctor, to acquiesce forever to the gross and demean-
ing features that she had been given, perhaps this would have been
a different story. Perhaps I would have grown to love someone who
would accept me as I was. But she was at that bank to deposit the
money for the surgery that you had sold her, Doctor.

   "So . . ." Patricia had waited, unruffled, for me to read the good-
bye letter.

   "It says the carrier of the letter will come to visit if she has any
need of my aid and—"

   "I know what it says," interrupted the selfsame carrier. "What
I'm interested in is if you're going to help."

   "That depends," my throat answered, but I already knew I
wouldn't do it. By allowing a woman such as Patricia to meddle in
my life, to come to my doorstep, to read my correspondence, Alicia
had betrayed the pact of our intimacy. I wondered if she had really
recognized me that day at the bank or if it was all just a trick to
get me to hide her away at my house during the week before the
operation. It was true that she had opened that post office box for

me abroad—a delicate mission I could not have entrusted to anybody else. That was true. But hadn't I, on the other hand, destroyed
all her files so she could leave the country without being arrested,
when someone—do you know who I'm talking about, Doctor?—
turned a picture of her most recent face over to the police? So we
were even. I owed her nothing.

"I have someone whom I'd like you to keep. Just for a night.
She's . . . a friend."

I could read her panic. What an actress—Patricia; what a performance: she was the kind who doesn't need to study a role in front
of the mirror, the dangerous kind who ends up believing her own
lies. But nobody sewed *my* eyelids together. Her serenity was as
false as her words, as false as her name. If I felt like it, one of these
days I'd drain you like a gutter, Patricia, I'd unfasten every button
in your life, I'd leave you with nothing more than a smear of skin
to hide in. Thank Alicia, whose memory still protects you—or I
would capture you, each inch of your garbage. Your most undesir-
able and indecorous moment would be put out to dry in my darkroom, and then I would send you to join all the other photos in
that post box Alicia herself rented for me abroad. I abstained from
prowling out Patricia's motives, from anticipating, as I always do
when somebody intrigues me, a past, a probable biography. Her
schemes did not interest me. I was, in fact, beginning to feel bored.
It was time to polish the whole matter off.

"Impossible," I said.

"There's no danger," Patricia lied.

"Then you take care of her."

"I can't."

"And why can I?"

"Alicia told me that . . . you were special. That nobody would
ever think of looking in your house."

"Alicia told you that?"

"It's only for a day. I'll come get her tomorrow. For sure."

"You won't need to come tomorrow. Or the day after, for that
matter. To be clear, don't ever come back. Not with your friend.
Not without her." I stood up: she could understand this was no
light decision. I passed her Alicia's photograph. I still hadn't looked
at it. "And take this with you. I won't be needing it."

Not knowing that two days later I would have that very Patricia, as insolent as ever, in front of me again, repeating the same bravura performance:

"Only for a night."

Strange that I should not be bothered by her duplicity, more visible now than the last time. If she left Oriana with me, she wasn't going to return tomorrow. Who knows how many days she had been trying to get the afflicted girl off her back. Maybe someone had stuck her with Oriana just the way she was trying to stick her with me now. That's how I perceived Oriana's life for months, deposited and transferred from house to house like a package. Until nobody knew who had her or who was responsible for collecting her again. I was, at any rate, the last stop. Because if Patricia, as seemed likely, did not return, I really didn't have any other place where I could leave the burden, not if these eyes of mine were unable to get themselves even one paltry witness in the whole universe, and with a witching doctor like you, Mivalleri, chasing the light out of them. That same reasoning should have moved me to repeat: "Impossible, impossible," to befuddle her with some stupid excuse, perhaps more rational than any the two of them had heard during these last endless days. No. There was no way she would be coming back tomorrow. Because if I was the last name on a list that had already failed her hour by hour, who was Patricia to obtain tomorrow? How could she sincerely guarantee that someone would relieve me of this prize so soon? That some one would ever relieve me? The panic, the weariness in Patricia's hands, not even trying to disguise themselves as something else, should have warned me.

Instead, as usual, I felt quite confident that I would be able to confront any problem that would develop. I could not deny that Patricia had not given me her real name, but on the other hand, she couldn't know that I had, that I still have, her face in my memory and that this could lead me to her more efficiently than any erasable smudge of fingerprints. If I had to locate her to return this piece of cargo, a quick consultation of my office files would be enough.

None of which I told Patricia when she stood up to say goodbye.

"There's something else," she said. "Don't let her out of the house, not for any reason. They're—well, somebody's looking for Oriana."

If I had had my camera in order to capture the crack of fear with which her face split open. It was only for a moment. What was inside her opened and shut as if a ray of light had sliced a block of ice and revealed, for less than an instant, the thing that had been caught, in there, dead and dying. What I saw in Patricia was more than that vague terror which from the start had been as noticeable as the sweat on her face. What she had allowed herself now, because she knew that I was going to take custody of the luggage called Oriana no matter what happened, was the image of her own ending. Someone was going to kill her. If I had that abyss of her face in a photo, I could have continued exploring it, asking questions of its gray areas, I could have questioned Patricia's corpse in order to extricate from her eyes that were setting the image of her murderers, and what they were hunting in Oriana. Because they were going to kill Patricia because of Oriana, due to something that Oriana was hiding, due to—it was my guess—something Oriana may perhaps not even have, anymore. But the ray of light passed and was swallowed up. And there was no more investigating I could do. Afterward I would lament my reluctance, but at the moment I found it unimportant. I thought that Oriana's past would be there, as always, on the surface of her skin—that I could suck it out of her as easily as a nurse's syringe draws blood from a body before an autopsy.

"What you should know, perhaps, is that—" Patricia began saying.

I admonished her with my hand. "Not a word. I don't want to know anything about her."

Patricia must have thought it was to protect myself, so I could pretend I didn't know anything in case Oriana was in real trouble. Patricia was wrong. What I wanted was to be able to find out who she was on my own, to follow her mysterious tracks without listening to information of any sort volunteered by anyone, true or false. I never wanted to feel, when I faced her, like the other inhabitants of this city, who, when they meet strangers, stock up on useless data, statistics, annotations, dental records, credit information, feigning a knowledge they do not have. I did not want ever to be like you, Doctor, when you submerge yourself inside the face of someone who intrigues you, unpeeling her enamel layer by layer, with all your technical contrivances and your implants and your X-rays and your incisions, all of you descending mercilessly upon your patients.

It was then that Patricia looked at me with a glint of doubt in her eyes.

"Say good-bye for me, will you? Tell her I'll come for her tomorrow—for sure."

And with these words, she left.

I am glad to be able to inform you, Doctor, that I have not seen her since. They must have killed her rather soon.

How did Oriana sit on the toilet?

It is not a trifling question, Doctor. If she were one of those women who wrinkles her skirt up till it presses in on her like an old strait jacket, her panties locking one knee to the other, and then proceeds to loosen a gush as narrow and miserly as those faces you operate, if she were one of those who wants to protect herself from the drafts of air and the eyes in the wallpaper, if she had been one of those, I wanted nothing to do with her. I required openness: getting rid of her skirt with a kick, tossing the panties away as if she would never use them again, absolutely delighted with the fluids that were about to drop from her body. I required her without fear.

To contemplate how a woman lets go on the toilet seat is one of the best ways, though not the only way, to avoid making a mistake with her.

In Oriana's case, destiny—or at least destiny with the sham name of Patricia—had offered me the perfect possibility of confirming that my intuition about her was correct. She had been banished to my own bathroom, no less, to await our decisions about her immediate future. All I had to do was drag my aching leg up the stairs with all necessary quietness and put one periscopic eye to the blessed keyhole, the best friend of every man who wants to discover the quicksands that women hide. What else are your operations, Doctor, other than an attempt to close that marvelous slot, to make sure that nobody will ever again be able to read the real face of one of your patients?

The fact that I did not give in to the temptation of spying on Oriana in the bathroom, the fact that I awaited her presence down-stairs, could almost be called an act of recklessness. Recklessness? I can already hear you, Mavrelli, making fun of me. Reckless? To respect the privacy of a guest? And yet, I was taking an enormous risk, breaking one of my most sacred customs. You know what I'm talking about, Doctor. You've boasted ponderously in newspapers that you could operate on anyone—even someone with no face, someone like me, unsalvageable. But if I were to appear to chal-lenge your claim, would you really risk it? I don't think so. And in my case, I was betting that Oriana was so absolutely different from other women I had known in my life that it would be worth approaching her in a different manner. What I was abandoning, in fact, was a method that, since my earliest days, had helped me to examine, one after another, an endless beehive of vixens, a method that had proved infallible.

I was six years old the first time I had ever decided not to apply such a profitable procedure, and it took me almost a decade to recover from the disastrous results. I was in love with a little girl called Enriqueta and, forgetting everything I had learned while squinting at my mother, sisters, cousins, aunts, or female family friends—following them as they discretely stood up to leave the room—against every instinct in my retinas, as a supreme token of adoration and trust of Enriqueta, I abstained. Temporarily, Doctor.

At the beginning, that abstention was the only homage I could pay her. I'll admit it is not the best way to win the heart of the pret-tiest girl in our class—the silent sacrifice of not watching her while she's pissing. But what other offering could I surrender?

Nobody paid any attention to me, and why should she, the most popular of all the girls I knew, with her wealthy parents, her father who was a doctor just like you, have been an exception? I was nothing, no one, less than one. Other than my furtive con-vergences upon the keyhole, I did not have, at the time, even one weapon with which to defend myself.

Photography? I had not yet realized the pleasures it would bring. And the fact that I was completely anonymous? I was aware—no doubt about it—that nobody remembered me, that the world acted as if I had not been born. Less visible than an Indian or a nigger, much less visible than one of those tramps sleeping in the street. At least people don't walk on one of those; they side step the smell from the shit glued to their unwashed asses. They take them into account. But not even that, for me. People I have known for years stumble against me, push me. If I'm lucky, they'll apologize: Oh, so sorry, they say, without the faintest show of familiarity, never able to tell who I am. One day, in front of our home, my own father gave me a shove. Not only did he not recognize me, on top of that he insulted me: "Why the fuck don't you watch where you're going?" Blaming me for his clumsiness.

I still had not fully understood that this semivisibility, my esteemed Doctor, could in other circumstances constitute an advantage. I would be able to circulate among people and find out each one of their secrets, follow my closest relatives, schoolmates, colleagues, and never be noticed. Later, when I had gained access to the state archives, to medical files, school report cards, confidential memos from insurance agents, not to speak of the inexhaustible documents of the Department of Traffic Accidents, it would have been easy to humble someone like Enriqueta, to add her to my collection.

But I was as defenseless as any child of six. More defenseless, because I had no knickknack to sell, no rhyme to recite, no cute song to trill. There was not in me even one smile with which to coax some dessert out of a mother or to blackmail an uncle into taking me to the movies. How was I to know how unusual it was to remember each intense face so well, each pimple and pore on each cheek, each soft or blustery mustache? I believed—and you know, Doctor, I may still believe—that all children have a similar talent. It may be that I had to preserve and develop mine because, unlike other children, I had no other skill with which to replace that natural aptitude everyone is born with.

For several months, I waited for the opportunity to render Enriqueta some unheard-of service: to gallop to the rescue, to save her from some ogre—someone like you, Doctor—who wanted to steal her face. And as such an occasion did not present itself, I decided to bribe her with a gift. Not an easy thing to do. I did not receive an allowance. When I asked for it, my father would assure me that it had already been given to me and that I was trying to cheat him. He had instantly contrived for himself some sort of ice-cold memory. That's how it always was with me: not only did people refuse to see me, but when I protested, they would cram me into their invented reminiscences so as to quickly get rid of me. I was inserted, over and over, into a past that they convinced themselves existed but that I had never lived. I was condemned, therefore, to manufacture the gift by myself.

I chose to send her some drawings, one each day. Double mistake. The first: I was unable to cross two lines in the right place, unable to close a wavering circle, unable to paint the colors of the rainbow without seeing them run like tears. A justifiable awkwardness. My hand anticipated instinctively what my eyes would discover someday: that only a photo does not lie. Or some photos, at least, Doctor. But that was not all. The drawings themselves were deceitful. Enriqueta was frivolous, cruel, merciless, but I pictured her as magnificent and benign, generous as a smiling sun. As if by merely describing her in this way, Malaveri, she would magically be converted into that person. Many years would pass before I realized that this sort of procedure, which plastic surgeons have perfected in order to capture people's souls, was of no use to me. Did I also want to impose upon a skin that did not deserve it the forgery of a beautiful mask? I had not learned a law that you certainly knew, Doctor, when you chose your profession: the more illusions you have about someone, the more captive you are. I was Enriqueta's prisoner. A prisoner without the right to enter her castle. Her castle? Not even the cellars of that castle.

If I began to send drawings to her, it was because I wanted to be invited to her birthday. No matter how unsightly those drawings might be, they were a way of asking for attention. Each morning, when she arrived at her desk, she found the gawky colors I had worked on so hard. It is true that she never thanked me for them, not even casting me one of those smiles which you fabricate, Doctor; but I comforted myself with the thought that she was receiving them like a remote queen who, however accustomed to the cheers of the multitude, nevertheless could feel gratified by an offering from a worm. Each morning she would put the drawing away in her schoolbag. If she was taking it home, it had to have some special value to her, and my hopes grew that I would receive, for the first time in my existence, proof that someone had noticed me. What I wanted, Doctor, if you allow the distinction, was not to go to the party so much as to be invited.

The only child in the class who did not get a dainty little card with seven pink elephants dancing on the cover was yours untruly.

So you can understand, Doctor, even Alicia—Alicia with her face like a moon's crater, with her leatherworks smell, with her voice like barbed wire on a record—even she had gotten an invitation. Strange how one can suffer, at that age, all the humiliations of the universe and still not give up. We seem to need more. Otherwise, why in heaven did I, the day of the party, having calculated that all the other children had already left, direct my shoes to scuffle toward Enriqueta's house? It wasn't that I had decided something as drastic as breaking my silent promise not to spy on her. It just turned out that way.

At the back of her garden, her father had built a playhouse for her. There was a watchdog, but I wasn't scared: not even the dogs bother to look at me. It was as if I were a stone for that mutt. I approached the playhouse slowly and, noticing a gap in the boards, I put my eye to it. The house was empty. In a corner, next to a pile of sprawling dolls, I saw my drawings, shipshape and intact. It was surprising that they should be there, as if they were being saved for some special occasion. Perhaps she was also in love with me but did not want to confess it. The idea that if someone loves you, she'll make you hurt—that sort of shit, Mirdovellez.

All of a sudden, I saw her come in, and instead of withdrawing my eyes, as my unilateral pact not to spy on her demanded of me, I stayed there, as if transfixed. Enriqueta was worn out, flushed from so much excitement. She was carting along a colossal doll, which seemed new—they had just bought it for her.

She sat it in front of a mirror and began to put make-up on its face. Those weren't play cosmetics she was using. Even at that age I knew more than enough about beauty products to realize that she had rifled her mother's boudoir.

I would never have dared do anything like that. My mother's powder and mascara were inviolable. Sitting in a babyseat in the mirrored room of the TV studio where the woman who had carried my unmemorable body inside her for nine months worked, only two years old, I figured out that cosmetics were not for me. If my mother was so busy preparing the businessmen, the politicians, the priests, the movie stars, for their interviews and banquets and debates, what sort of skin care was going to be left for her son? One face after the other, all afternoon and evening, painting the smile on one to deceive the other and the smile on the other to continue the deception and both smiles to deceive the fools in the audience, expending on her craft and clients all the time and tricks she never spent on me, not a speck of talcum, not an eyeliner, until one day I asked myself if my untouched face might be the reason no one ever paid any attention to me.

But all too soon I understood that not all the make-up in the world would have saved me. I understood it, to be precise, the day on which my little sister was born. I had encouraged the illusion that when she arrived she would fulfill two of my desires. The first was that she should have no face. And the second, that she should bring me mine, the one that had perhaps been forgotten back there, in those moist ashes inside my mother's stomach. But my sister was as complete as can be—bubbling over, pinkish—and brought me no other gift than the knowledge of my own loneliness. My mother, such an expert in the techniques of false eyelashes and wigs, did not need to wait so long. She must have guessed it instinctively in the instant of looking at me—or as she twisted her eyes away from me the first time. Unlike my brothers, I had nothing in my face that anybody could register, not a surface on which some improvement could be imagined, not the rag of a possible alteration. If someone like you, Doctor, a genius such as you, had seen me at the beginning, who knows if my life might not have changed. Or if some woman, many years later, Alicia perhaps, had given me birth with a permanent look instead of chasing the mirage of a face promised by the unhealing hands of the surgeons of this world.

What is certain is that the woman who should have succored me did not do so. That she brought me into the world, that lady who cloaked faces, of that there was no doubt. But she had not continued with me for the rest of the voyage. She left me there, featureless, abandoned on the wharf—or on the ship that was departing—and I had to defend myself alone. Because what is superimposed upon the blank blackboard children bring with them is their parent's face. That is why—and not for some stupid biological reason—they look more and more like their fathers and mothers as the years grow by. At birth, parents and relatives and lovers coo, flattering themselves with some conceivable resemblance. Lies. For a real similarity, mere fornication, pressing one seed into service so it becomes an unwilling body, is insufficient. In order to secure that face, the adult must keep on interposing himself between the just-born baby and the world. For the rest of its life the child will pay for that protection against alien eyes. You must know what I'm talking about, Doctor, you must have studied it scientifically.

The first face a little one sees is not something far away, outside, like a mirror in the sky. Not so. The first thing any child sees is the inside of his father's face, he sees the maneuvers that his own features must start rehearsing and that are constantly being sewn onto him like an umbrella of skin against the rain. In order to keep out other, possibly worse, invaders, he adopts his father's shell. Human beings are trapped inside the dead faces of their remote ancestors, repeated from generation to generation. From inside that chain, the grandparents of our grandparents watch us. Adults are their envoys, Doctor, the incessant, invisible remodelers of each baby born. So what every child inspires in the world is not a blessing, but a face lift. Every child, that is, except for me.

I do not know if I was born without a face or if I refused to fashion one—refused to do to myself what Enriqueta was at that very moment doing to her doll. By then I already knew, as I watched her, that each morning adults compose their shields for the day, the walls they will inflict upon children and anybody else in the hours to come. I was tiny, I could hardly walk, I think, when I would get up on full-moon nights and toddle to my parents' room to watch them sleep. At times I saw them making love. I wasn't scared. Even if they had lifted their eyes, even if later on they had awoken, they wouldn't have seen me. It was the faces that flickered on them during their nightmares that captivated me, the only faces that were not spruced up, the only faces without a mother—mine or any other—to intervene at dawn, without an inner plastic surgeon preparing the façade as the body's ambassador. There was no insurance agent in those faces, no selling of them in the stock exchange or the futures market of everyday life. Doctor, there are no fairy godmothers. They don't exist. But stepmothers of your body, yes, there are those, Doctor, reconstructing at the moment of awakening our daily mask, defeating the truths that the night has permitted the brain to distill, our daily looks, amen. Watching Enriqueta's rouge-stained doll, I understood that what I had needed was a loving hand to shed upon me a benediction of colors. I was born without a surgeon godfather—and no mother to furnish my lips with flowers for the day's long funeral. The woman who had spawned me was too busy with the faces of strangers to make that special effort to rescue me, and so I sunk ever more into anonymity.

Enriqueta lay her cosmetic-slurred doll on a small cot and took out a series of medical instruments from a bag—these, at least, were playthings. She shook the baby to make it cry, and when a broken, almost human, hiccup sputtered up, "My little love," Enriqueta lullabied. "Are you sick?"

She set about to discover—the daughter of a doctor, after all— what was wrong with the doll. She sounded it and pinched it and scratched its underarms brutally; she explored the nasal channels with a flashlight and the eardrums with a little hammer. I had been through that—the medical exams. My father sold medical equipment to hospitals: hypodermic needles, stethoscopes, things that penetrate the body and try to emerge with a representation of what is happening inside. I had heard him talk about something called an X ray, which took photographs of people's innards. I wondered if maybe those photos might reveal why nobody paid any attention to me, if they would reveal that something was wrong. In order to get them taken, I faked tremendous tummy pains—which had the added advantage of allowing me to go to the bathroom ten, eleven times, each day and to spy on whomsoever was in it while I awaited my turn outside.

When the results were brought in, I was disappointed. Sorry to have to tell you this, Doctor—for you, after all, those plates are like maps, the secret topography onto which you graft your false buildings. But believe me—and you may agree with me here—that gray rubbish, those inert shadows, those sterile ghosts, were anything but the truth. They were just as much a sham as the knuckles of doctors drumming on one's thorax, guessing at the dark, sick light that lodges in our lungs. I aspired to different depths, depths that everyone can see. That was not me on those negatives. Because in there, in our intestines, we are all equal. So are frogs fried dry by the sun. Trying to find the difference between human beings in the bones—what madness. What each of us really means rises to the surface, yes, right there, for everybody to see—or would you disagree, Doctor? There is a hidden something that will at any moment emerge and will pose itself, just so, Moravelli, like a blister on a mouth that is about to be punctured, and if you happen not to be present, if you do not know ahead of time that this supreme moment is on the verge of briefly blossoming, then that truth will submerge itself all over again. But it will surge outward once more, it will, no matter how much people such as you try to cover it or suffocate it or whatever it is that you do to it.

Was that when I began to hate doctors, the day I was shown those plates? No, I hated them long before that. I think that I portended that you would be my great rival, Doctor Marviralle, that you would be awaiting me in the future, ready to practice to its utmost that capacity for camouflage that people learn from their parents, ready to fling counterfeit faces in my direction to see if I would be able to decipher them. The instinctive hatred of plastic surgeons—the worst of the lot, because they do not even respect the outer trimmings, because all their efforts are made in order to suppress a revelation. Not that the others are any better, with their god of pills, their smell like a pharmacist's thumbs, believing that they can sound out what moves slowly in our depths, inserting their instruments into the mouth and beyond the asshole and under the fingernails, into the swamp of a heart we have each inherited. Cleavers that open you as if you were a can of food. To open, to open, to make you bleed, to enter and then—what? Then, nothing. Then they proclaim that they have discovered what is corrupting us, when they are the ones responsible for having made us sick in the first place. That's their strategy—to make people suffer, just as Enriqueta was now making the doll suffer, in order to explore a sickness that was no more real than the one I had feigned, and all so that the patients would be grateful. A smile from the doll, because Enriqueta's left hand was now beginning to give comfort for what her own right hand had been visiting upon it.

Enriqueta sang to the doll in a throaty voice. I allowed something inside me to feel—perhaps for the last time—devastated by the promise of tenderness, the illusion that she would hum this to a child of mine or, better still, directly to me. That zone inside me that listened to the song, was that the section of my being, the clefts of my eyes, that could recognize the seductive force of music, that had the capacity to listen to melodies, but that later on began to close down on me? How can I know? It may be possible that the lullaby of a woman like Enriqueta could have awoken those sounds in my optic nerves. If so, what my eyes witnessed immediately cut off that possibility forever: Enriqueta began to feed the doll with a bottle. The substance inside was wormlike and white, as if someone had mixed dust, lime, even some milk. She poured it into the doll's mouth and lifted its dress and took off its underpants. Then I saw how she sat it down on a tiny mock toilet seat.

And then I realized why Enriqueta was taking my drawings home. I knew it before I had to watch how the flow of that liquid mix tapered from the doll's meager underbelly, I knew it before I had to see the hand of the woman whom I had just been dreaming of as my mate for life snake toward the stock of drawings and . . . It wasn't that she used my homages to her as toilet paper. If she had used them for her own rivulets and apertures, I might have convinced myself that she was attempting at least some form of intimacy. But the doll. I swore that one day I would . . . I would what? What would I do to her? What would I do with my life?

Of the years that followed, Doctor, the six, seven years that followed, I do not even want to evoke a memory. If I had been able to brand that doll's dirty bottom forever in my mind, if I had been able to bring it to my eyes without time's destroying it, as it destroys and menstruates everything, if I could have kept intact that pure implacable flame of hatred I felt . . . Memory is always a fraud—erased, manipulated, sweetened by somebody, somebody always swearing it was some other way until you are not sure yourself. The past is like one of those faces captured by hands such as yours, Doctor—always subject to alterations. Standing in front of adults, how many times had I desired to return to the past, where I had been so humiliated, to prove to myself that my resentment was no fantasy. It was impossible to go back, impossible to free myself from those older people. Instead, I had to submit, I had to cast down my discolored eyes. Equally impossible, I thought, to bring that piece of the past to my own present. If I could have done that, a girl like Enriqueta would never again confuse me with a giggle—not Enriqueta, not anybody else, would ever again make me drunk with her pretty face. It was too easy for her to recapture me with the foreplay of her illusory lips. A bulwark, that's what I needed—a bulwark against time.

I did not know yet that what I was looking for was nothing other than a photograph.

Meanwhile, Mentirelli, I had no better defense against people than to become more submissive, to await someone's remote generosity and to start licking his shoe. It was the lap dog's hope of nuzzling into the nook of somebody's affections. But not even a speck of dust bothering an eyelid, not even a draft that makes you get up to shut the door—I was less than those things to them. I was trapped in the worst of dependencies: at the mercy of someone else's love. Leftovers from other smiles, the residue of a happiness meant for another, the last floating particle in a universe without its own light. Darkness, the darkness of those years in the basement of somebody else's mind. A candy bar in an old shop where no one buys anything, anymore, a candy bar which always remains for some reason in even next year's stock, which grows stale, which is on sale and discounted over and over again, until it goes for free and still nobody wants it, not even a beggar would touch it. Clearance sale and everything is sold, except that item. There I am, waiting for anyone, in the empty shop that the carpenters begin to dismantle. Nobody to take me home. Nobody to take me to some plastic surgeon so I could grow the face I needed.

The long blankness of those years before I got my camera: humiliations that were all the worse because nobody actively desired them. I lived as if I were missing. The teachers were surprised when I returned my written tests—as if, for an instant, they realized that I did exist, the brief flash of a match light against the horizon, as if, for an instant, I would appear like a satellite on the sky of their conscience, with only the purpose of quickly setting, my days in their conscience instantaneously created and immediately extinguished. Surprised that I was in their class, because they never spoke to me or asked me a question, they never expelled me, they never called on my uplifted hand. Anybody sitting next to me at the cafeteria was always talking to the kid on the other side. What I would have given, like a used-up cigarette butt, for someone to have put me to their lips for a last—or in my case, a first—puff. For someone to put their lips to the ashes of my lips.

I had decided—although I doubt it could really be called a decision, Doctor, it was more of an inevitable conclusion—to live like this for the rest of my mediocre existence. When, at the age of twelve, perhaps thirteen, my organ for what is called love began to grow, when that part of my body rebelled and did not want to accept the solitude to which the rest of my being had resigned itself, I asphyxiated it. It stretched out with hunger, it filled with rampaging blood, it hardened against my hand and my skin, which were trying to pacify it. No moist sponge with soap would do, no reproductions of the Venus of Milo, no promises of dolls like Enriqueta's. It had to be Enriqueta herself. Enriqueta or nobody.

And it would have been, undoubtedly, nobody, if the art of photography had not come to my rescue at just about that time.

Each year there was some stupid family reunion, which culminated in an equally imbecilic final ceremony: the neighbor would come by, all false benevolence, to act as official photographer. Which is precisely why photography held no interest for me—because it had always been the authoritative voice of the adult world, the collector of discardable memories. Another cheater of the senses, a new falsifier of time past so that people would not have to make the effort to remember it as it really had been. The worst make-up trick of all. I felt this so strongly that I do not appear in any family album—or in any photo, for that matter. I cannot tell, Doctor, if that is due to my own sneaking away, preferring to be a spectator of the others' deluded quest for immortality; or if it was the camera itself which understood that my function was not to be snarled into a photograph but to photograph someone else, and which therefore automatically excluded me from the panorama it was taking.

So when the neighbor let us know at the last moment that he could not come that day and the family had to search for a replacement, I didn't mind that they chose me. I patiently waited while they carried out a typical adult discussion among hypocrites. They all wanted to be in the photo and offered to sacrifice their interest so that the others would say no, and finally, as I expected, one of them—it must have been my mother—said, But he (she would not even deign to pronounce my name), but he won't mind. Of course. Why should I mind?

They all got into the appropriate positions.

I snapped some seven shots, one after the other, as if I were drugged. Okay, they said, that's enough. I did not obey. It was as if a couple about to explode in an orgasm was asked to cease their movements. As they disbanded, I went on pressing the camera's button, gorged inside the camera's gigantic sexual eye, throbbing madly inside that camera. I kept on pressing the button and still was pressing it spasmodically when there was no more film. I had to stuff into the sweet cavern of that black machine all my memories just as I was seeing them.

My mother was red with anger. "Look at this spendthrift. He's wasted the whole roll." She was angrier still, some days later, when she had the photos developed. The seven of the family were clouded over, as if a paraplegic had taken them. "This brat can't do anything right."

And the others?

My mother waved her hand in disgust. "Dreadful."

"Let me see."

"You are not going to see anything. We're—why, we're . . . ugly. Horrible, if you must know. As if somebody had spat us out."

"Let me see, Mom."

"Everything this brat does comes out wrong. This'll be the first family gathering we won't have a photograph of."

To punish me, she didn't even let me peek at them. I saw those claws of hers tearing up each photo, grinding them, searching out the weakest part of the paper—and sending all the pieces to the garbage.

That night I went down to retrieve my photographs. As if I were apprenticed to some plastic surgeon, Doctor, I spent several days putting the pieces together again. Sloppy with strands of squash, frying oil, peelings, buttered over with foul-smelling salad dressing, punctured by pork bones. I felt no revulsion. For years I had been salvaging food from plastic bags. I was an expert in junk.

But even I did not know enough to recompose all those mustard-stained photos. A mirror that has cracked and is repaired can never give out the same light as a normal mirror. There were the faces I remembered, devastated by the acid in my mother's fingers, washed by my cousins' gastric juices, sickened by sauces for a banquet to which I was never invited. But none of that could stop me from realizing that these photographs were marvelous. Not the ones clouded over, the official ones. The other ones, where my relatives had been caught off guard.

I went through them and over them and into them with a love that was infinite. Once again I felt the total joy I had contracted at the moment when I had pressed that button. They corresponded exactly, shade by shade, to the image I still kept in my head. I knew that if I had them now, without a tear, without a stain, they would have been the exact and mathematical replica of what I had seen through that magic eye in the howling instant when the button had clicked. More than that, I knew that if I was the owner of a camera, I would be able to reach the most absolute harmony between my brain and the world. There it was, confirmed in something alien to me, a shining sheet of broken celluloid—the evidence.

I had found my calling.

And had simultaneously lost the instrument that would allow its fulfillment.

Because my parents never again loaned me the camera. Still less would they have thought of buying me one. I have wondered if their denial was due to their having realized that the photographs my mother had destroyed were dangerous. Did they catch a glimpse of themselves as they really were? And could they not bear that someone, in particular their own son, would journey through the world with a machine that captured the black nakedness in their soul, in each person's soul? Did they understand instinctively, as I did, that if I had been able to keep intact that proof of their vileness and hypocrisy, I would have entangled them forever in my eyes, that I would have been able to seize them and hold them ransom-less forever? Probably not: they were too arrogant to suppose that a nonentity such as myself would be able to do anything of the sort. Their denial was merely to punish me for having called attention to my existence, for having bothered them with my presence.

"It would be a waste of good money," my father had declared. "Like giving an armless man a piano."

To complicate matters, I didn't want just any camera. I needed the best equipment in the world. And a darkroom that I could use without any interference: so that nobody would ever again be able to tear up what I had seen. I was going to have to acquire these things, plus an abundant supply of virgin film, all on my own. Like everything I have ever gotten in life. Without anyone else's help.

It took me almost three years.

I had to tell myself to be patient. I silenced the galloping needs of my sex with the primitive, undeniable certainty that Enriqueta already belonged to me.

That prediction was to be verified to my complete satisfaction. To own another human being, the only thing necessary is to kidnap her intimacy, to deflower with my camera what my eyes had already explored. But initially my intuition about the future was still darkened by an illusion that continued to prey upon me. Normality. That illusion. Yes, I still dreamt of betrothing Enriqueta, of becoming my parents' prodigal son, of arriving with fanfare at a party. In a word, I was still submitting myself to the fiction that it was possible, and even desirable, for me to become permanently visible, a loyal member of your world, Doctor, the world where you reign.

Three years later, when the camera's hidden premiere deprived Enriqueta of her façade, I began to realize that I might be mistaken. And one week after that, when my sex had its own avid premiere inside the slime between Enriqueta's legs, I confirmed that the quest for normality was definitely a mistake.

Of course those people started to flutter their eyes on my forgettable face. Of course Enriqueta, as soon as I had gathered the evidence of her falsehood, as soon as the collection of her most abject moments were in my hands, gave herself up to me. But when she took off her clothes and her nakedness turned out to be less exciting and far less splendid than the photograph of her that I had slipped underneath my bedroom wallpaper, I grasped that making love to her was not going to liberate me. As long as I was obsessed with the need that she, that others, register my features in their fragile, blind contact lenses, as long as I had no other objective in life, I would continue to be chained to an orbit whose primary was someone else. Did I want to live the rest of my life extracting love from other people as if I were milking a cow? What value could her glance at me have if it depended on something as transitory as a photograph, if it was produced by her primitive, inexplicable fear of the photograph that she did not even know existed but that gave me power over her? What value is that, if she forgot me immediately?

If I wanted to be permanently recognized, I would have to live like a hypnotizer among his victims—forcing them to look at me, violating them at every turn, pulling at their leashes, devouring them with my eyes so that they would obscurely apprehend that I had somehow gotten into their bloodstream, that there was no recourse against that sort of transfusion. If, on the other hand, I wanted only to know them, then I could know them better than they could themselves, I could know the image that no mirror would dare reveal, I could penetrate deeper than any hypodermic needle, microscope, or X-ray machine, or the hands of a plastic surgeon. And deeper, I thought, at the very moment when I entered into Enriqueta, deeper and better than this sad vulnerable sex depositing its vomit inside uncaring muscles.

For one last time I tried to fool myself. I closed my eyes while I was making love, aware that I would open them upon the trembling of her orgasm. There she was, sweating love underneath me—a twisted image of herself. If she had managed to accede to that secret face of hers that I had crammed inside the photograph, if in the act of love she had been able to rise into her real identity, a flash of herself, a revelation, I could have forgiven all the other thousand impassive faces with which she had ground me into nothingness during the last decade; I might even have put aside that shameful moment with the doll. It might, perhaps, have been possible for my sex to verify her hidden face. But only my camera had that skill. There was no hope. She was as false in love as she was in everything else—the contortions of her rapture were mere propaganda, one more attempt to mock whoever might be watching her. What need was there of going through the obscene rite of entering and leaving her body with a piece of my own body if what she revealed was murkier and less passionate than what existed in my black-and-white celluloid collection?

This does not mean that I ceased using my own rather demanding organ. I religiously carried out the terms of the covenant we had subscribed to: he had been quiescent all the long years it took me to procure the photographic equipment that could satisfy his longings, and it was now my turn to serve at his pleasure. But it was a pleasure localized in the sad trigger itself, a pleasure that never fulfilled its threat of flooding the rest of my body with the violence of hot, remote waves, that could never compare with the total jubilation of a pair of eyes sucking the truth from a picture. You get me, Doctor, the jubilation of gnawing piece by piece the secrets that those women did not even tell their best friends. What a sense of well-being, to have inverted the roles at last: to act toward those women as if I were the visible one and they were the blind shadows. Sex ended up being no more than a trivial pursuit: far less interesting than the game I played with each face; inventing a history for it and then spending weeks researching the woman whose face it was, finding out how faithfully my imagination had constructed her story. That's why I turned my back on Alicia when she chose her artificial face. I did not want to risk the disappointment of seeing her cheeks glow with falsehood at the culminating moment of love-making. I did not want to steal her face from her or keep it forever in a photograph.

And that was also why, years later, I did not want to spy on Oriana; I would not treat her as I had treated the other women before her. She was the first woman in the world I did not fear. The first I would not have to photograph in order to coax an erection from my body.

"Oriana? Oriana, do you need something?"

She'd been in the bathroom for about half an hour and not a sound could be heard. Had something happened to her?

"Yes." Her answer came quite faintly through the door.

"You need something?"

"Permission."

"Permission for what?"

"Where's Patricia?"

"Patricia left. She said she'd be back tomorrow to get you."

"Then you're the one who'll have to give me permission."

This little game didn't bother me at all. It was a matter of putting my ear to the door and licking in the sound of her breathing on the other side, her body pulsating, itself drawn up to the wood. After so many years in which my eyes had been the only king of my body, there was a strange calmness in allowing them to rest. "I've never given something without getting something in return," I said.

"What do you want me to do?"

"You could start by telling me your real name."

"My real name?"

"Don't go and tell me that you're called Oriana. I don't know anybody called Oriana."

"And if I can't tell you my real name, you won't give me permission?"

"Did Patricia forbid it?"

"No. It isn't that. It's that . . . but you wouldn't believe me."

"Tell me and I'll give you permission."

"Promise that you'll believe me."

"Why shouldn't I?"

"If I told you, for example, if I told you that I didn't know, what would you say?"

"That you didn't know your own name?"

"If I don't know it, you won't give me permission?"

"Let's compromise. I'd settle for your nickname. They must have called you something when you were a kid, right?"

"I'm not going to speak one more word to you till you open this door."

All of a sudden I realized that this was the permission that, in Patricia's absence, she was expecting from me: permission to come out of the bathroom! Some laceration in the echo of her voice indicated to me—and I was not seeing her—that for her our playful interchange had never been a game.

"You open it," I said. "I'm not the one who's got you shut up inside."

"You'll give me permission to open it?"

"Yes."

"Even if I don't tell you my name."

"I'll give you all the permissions in the universe."

"No. You open it."

I opened the door.

Where did that air of innocence come from? I don't believe it was the smile, ripe, full as her lips. Or that cascade of savage hair, which somehow contained the mouths that had passed through it, tasting it. Not even those eyes, in which, in spite of the lack of one lonesome tear, there shone a moist forlornness, as if something in her, very far away, had been crying.

She stretched her arms upward, as children do when they want to be carried or comforted.

I didn't want to think about it, I didn't want to, but it was inevitable—corrupting the moment, soiling it from the past.

That's right, Doctor. It was that damn doll of Enriqueta's that intercepted my memory at that very moment. As abandoned as Oriana was now, I demanded in that silence some sort of proof that it was really me those arms were begging for to save her, now that she was in distress—not Patricia, not some other man, not a doctor to the rescue, but me. I demanded proof that her eyes would not pass through me as though I did not exist.

I awaited a signal that I was the one she needed.

It came.

For the second time in one hour, perhaps in my life, I saw myself reduced to what my ears could apprehend in order to decipher the maps of the universe. From somewhere—but it had to be from inside her, from the darkness in her stomach, which had just had breakfast, which had recently oozed some element into my toilet as a sign of trust while I did not spy upon her—the slightest of laments slit the air to remind me of all that we already shared, a wail from her innerside which sounded, clearly, as a song for me. An invitation to invade the place where no eye could ever go and no camera roam—someplace warm and turbulent and digesting and murmuring inside her—a place which was, which had to be, for me.

I gathered her into my arms.

"It's just that"—and her breath tickled my neck, made my hair stand up as if it had been charged with electricity—"it's that . . . It's not as if I didn't want to tell you. My name. It's just that I don't remember."

"You don't remember?"

And when she answered, Doctor, there dawned in me the beginning of an understanding of what it was in her that attracted me so, though you won't believe me. I began to see how it was possible that a person who didn't have so much as a stain to hide, could simultaneously be one loud howl demanding exploration, the beginning of an explanation.

"I don't remember that or anything else."

The next question, the automatic next and decisive question—I was unable to ask it, because suddenly, like an injection piercing directly to the nerve, like the claw of some surgeon intersecting my eardrums, the doorbell rang. Once again somebody was bothering me on a holiday at my own home.

"Don't open."

Nor was that fear a lie, that murmur on my cheek, those trembling arms which wouldn't let me go. I had no intention of opening it, but I wanted to measure her reaction: "Why not?"

"Maybe it's them."

"Them."

For an instant it was like being in front of Patricia all over again, like watching, again, an iceberg penetrated by an infection of light, again seeing the image of a dead woman in the backdrop of her terror. But this time the victim was Oriana and not Patricia. What did those men seek in Oriana? They wanted her voice filled with blood. They wanted her voice never to tell certain things.

I deplored, for the first time, my lack of foresight. I had let go, without chasing it, the image Patricia had opened to me, let go of the shadows that could reveal what those men were looking for in Oriana's throat. What is deposited in a throat? Melodies? Memories? Stories? Words that others are scared of keeping? Had they been given over to Oriana so she could keep them? And her amnesia, was it precisely a way of trying to avoid those men? So that, if they ever found her, they would not be able to slowly drain from her the memories she had accumulated? If there had been time to explore her before someone downstairs, maybe one of those very men that . . .

"Them?" I asked once more, to see if that shook her memory.

"Patricia can tell you."

"And if it's Patricia who's come to get you?"

She put a finger to my lips: Hush, hush, her fingers said. "She's not that gentle when she knocks."

"But if it were Patricia?"

"She doesn't need me, anymore."

"Whereas I . . ."

"You'll be better at taking care of me. But why talk, anymore: it isn't her."

It wasn't.

Because all of a sudden we heard the door open and the placid footsteps of a man and then, out of the silence, the voice of Tristan Pareja, calling to me.

It was partly my fault: I had called Pareja that very morning. But if the bitch Patricia hadn't left the door unlatched . . .

"It's my lawyer," I grumbled into Oriana's ear.

"Make him go away."

"I can't. I need him."

"What for?"

"I'll tell you later."

"Tell me now."

Downstairs, Pareja's voice could be heard ever louder. I heard one of his shoes creaking on the stairs. He was coming up!

"Coming, I'm coming," I yelped, trying to feign sleepiness. And to her, barely above a murmur: "They're going to catch us. You want them to catch us? Then into that room. Right away. That one. At the end of the hall."

"Be careful," she said, giving me a quick kiss on my neck, moist as a bird flying from the rain. "He might be one of them."

And she started off down the corridor to my bedroom.

I grabbed one of her hands and drew her toward me. The swiftness with which she had obeyed me when so much authority had crept into my voice resurrected for me that question I had been on the point of asking when the buzzer interrupted us. But first I said to her, "Don't you dare come down until I give you permission. Understand?"

She nodded.

And after that the question that now, more than ever, was burning up my mouth:

"How old are you, Oriana? Or are you going to tell me you don't know that, either?"

I was not so surprised by her answer. A suspicion had been swirling in my head since I was bowled over by her as soon as I saw her. But it still was difficult to believe that purring, indignant, luxurious voice of hers when it announced:

"Of course I know how old I am. I'm four years old." But she ended up by convincing me when she added, with her eyes unsullied by the slightest shadow of a lie, "But I'll be celebrating my fifth birthday next month."

You haven't got a partner, Mavirelli. No need to be a genius to find that one out. I may no longer commandeer, for now, perhaps for some time to come, the channels through which I would usually have investigated an interloper, even one so familiar as you; so I merely looked it up in the phone directory. There you are, replete with all your titles, but without an associate. I don't blame you: to submerge oneself in the water that stagnates beneath a stranger's face, it is best to be alone.

You could afford the luxury. Though I was more lonely, I couldn't. I've got a—all right, right, I can see your smile, Miravello, if you had heard me using the verb in the present tense, so I'll correct myself; during many years I had, yes, as you well know, I used to have a partner. I procured him when it became essential to obtain the money for the camera. Even if I had not been cursed by my singular condition of semivisibility, the sort of business I was setting upon would have demanded it. Dangerous trade. But I could think of no other way to produce long-term dividends. I might have been young, but I already understood how vital it was that nobody should ever guess the power that these eyes of mine bestow upon me. You know what? I still think the same thing today: if people were to suspect who I am, they would liquidate me. Even you, with all the spies you have on my tail, do not begin to surmise what I hide. Soon, though, you will find out.

Unlike those who get involved with a partner blindly, commending themselves to fluctuating laws and ineffectual contracts to protect them from mistrust, mockery, and theft, I had, my cunning Doctor, an advantage. I could examine the defects of my schoolmates, one by one, till I discovered the right person. And I could take all the time required. Not only that. The more time I took, the deeper I foraged into their lives—and naturally into the lives of our teachers—the more profitable my business. Not a dirty closet, not a furtive nose picker, not a concealed perversion, escaped me. They had treated me as if I did not exist; this was vengeance of a scrupulous nature, to use my insignificance to witness their animal grunts as they learned the first steps of sex, the sounds that came from them as they lost control over their shaking bodies. Oh, yes: without knowing it, they defiled themselves every night in front of an audience of one.

The person I needed had to be my reverse, a human being absolutely befuddled by the urgency to be loved. Perhaps someone who many years ago had started out from the same gray indifference that others showed me but who had overcome it by other methods, who had chosen to gain affection by doing tricks, as if the world were a circus and his life had been created in order to entertain the spectators. Someone supposedly benevolent, a great jokester, whom nobody would ever suspect. Someone whom everybody liked a little bit but who really, deep inside (my eyes followed him there, even though I hadn't yet the film with which to fix his excesses), hated all those around him. The essence of resentment, someone who—with the hope of piling up a something of money and an anything of fame—had become a pleasant-enough fellow, a garden of fraudulent smiles.

That person's name was Tristan Pareja, and to me he owes everything he has conquered in life.

He was the one who was going to be the front for my ambitions. It was a matter of playing upon the cords of his real ambition, giving him a mirror in which he would be able to recognize his most intimate longings—and then of waiting. The genie of the magic lamp, or the demon, could not have shown more patience than I. It was slow in developing: let him take the bait every week, swallow it over and over, until his gizzard was so full of hooks and lures that it would be enough to pull serenely on the string and I would have him gasping at my feet.

I began by sending him information. Every Monday a new tidbit. Though he had no idea who the source was, the information was shattering in its precision. He might have been a buffoon, but he was at least a clever buffoon. I watched him carefully so that I could be present when he decided to employ one of my messages to some purpose. And one day I saw how Tristan paralyzed the class bully with a phrase that was apparently innocent but that referred to the fact that the bastard had been masturbating on the principal's desk after hours. While my camouflaged face silently observed the bully's twitchings and moans. I almost felt like congratulating Tristan. That was the way to do things. Subtly, administering what you find out about others to gain ascendancy over them, without making them panic, letting them love you and speak well of you, controlling them so they don't realize. I felt even better about my choice when I garnered that Tristan was preparing his campaign to be class president. I kept on tossing him handy morsels, each week for months, until one day I dared suggest to him that we meet after class. He agreed, of course—he was hunting for votes—but I measured his perplexity: I could see how he probed his memory to find some trace of me, and came away with none.

He was even more startled when that very afternoon I told him that standing in front of him was none other than his informant. He wasn't ready to believe me. I mentioned a couple of incidents in his life, confidential and embarrassing, which only he knew, or at least, that is what he had thought up till this moment. About how he listened to his mother's menstrual pains, how he took her underwear out of the wash. About the neighbor's shaggy dog. Then he believed me. But never fully. He always supposed that someone was behind me, that I was fronting for someone just as he was fronting for me, a chain of hidden manipulators. It strikes me even now, thirty or so years later, that he still underestimates me, looks down on me. How could somebody as insignificant as I, less substantial than a shadow, be able to acquire so much vicious and verifiable gossip about people? I'm not bothered that he may think that: I even stimulate and encourage it.

At first, Tristan was insulted by my demand that he begin to use my information to get money. People are like that. You propose what they need, what should be absolutely clear to them, and it takes them weeks to accept it. They've got— I'm not sure if this is the right word, Doctor, because I have never felt anything like it—qualms, I guess. They need time to subdue what they call their conscience. Ridiculous to spend so much energy denying something that you're going to end up doing, anyway. Tristan was souring his life with a false squeamishness. He resisted selling the news I had been giving him. Poor thing must have thought that I had constructed my whole spy network merely so that he could be named the most popular kid in school.

"How can you ask me to blackmail my own friends?"

"Blackmail?"

The truth is that the idea had never come near my eyes. Not even now do I concur with that sort of tactic. But this photo, you'll say, the one that shortly you will have in your sweltering hands? And this demand of mine for a couple of favors? Not blackmail, Doctor. It's called war reparations: what a vanquished person, in this case you, Doctor, pays the victorious army.

I was against blackmail then, just as I am now, for reasons that had nothing to do with ethics: simply a matter of security. Nothing is riskier than offering to silence insinuations about someone in exchange for cash. They'll end up seeking revenge. Or, if they're too scared for that, they'll steal or commit some other crime to get some impossible sum, and when one of them is caught, as is bound to happen, the whole building comes tumbling down. You clean up today, you're broke tomorrow. Blackmail is a fundamentally unstable system, which can bring only ruin to all those involved.

It's much better to sell that secret information to others. That's what the press moguls have done—the inexpensive sale to curious mobs of what is unknown. To establish an extended net of prying minds and hook them with the sort of bait that I fed to Tristan; to reel in a couple of coins at a time, slowly, very slowly. Don't call attention to yourself, don't provoke catastrophes or melodramas. Instruct them about things they themselves could unearth if they were more observant, less vociferous, more ubiquitous. Satisfy their mania for trivia—what smudge-colored hairs that girl begins to tuft between her thighs, the fact that Carlos secretly wants to play in Jorge's position on the team and the maneuvers he's exercising to get his way, how long it takes the language teacher to evoke a whimper from the school secretary on their couch. The breasts of that secretary, the damp stain of her nipples, the way in which she calls the name of her uncle at the climax. I'd have made a great journalist, I think, but I'd have screwed myself. Better to be like this, behind the crowd, far from the madding eyes. Nobody was jealous of me. Nobody threatened me. Until I met up with you, Doctor Marvirelli.

So Tristan was refusing to cooperate with me. I had anticipated that sort of reaction. I knew that, within a couple of weeks, he would return with his mouth watering, to beg for a new crop of malice. People are trapped by what others start to expect of them; trapped, my dear Doctor, you who are such an expert in pigmentation, by the image they themselves have tried to introduce into everybody else's pupils. Do you understand now why I am a slave to no one?

Although, I'm really not sure if others fail to perceive me or if, one fraction of a second after my face interferes with their horizon, a millionth of a second after they have cast their gaze upon me, they already begin to wash me from their memory: forgotten before arriving at the scant, sad archangel of a remembrance. It's all the same how it happens. We require somebody to look at us in order to exist. As nobody can imagine me or even conjecture the possibility that I may be present, as this mistake that I turned into should not be there in front of their eyes, as it is clear to me that my mother should have aborted and maybe did, as my father instead of opening a bottle of champagne at my birth overlooked my existence and went to sleep, because of all this, since then, since before then, I have been an erasure. Everybody will go through this process of disappearance, once dead. I am the only one who has had to experience it while still alive.

That was why there was no risk in my witnessing the multiple couplings and treacherous entanglements that others call love. Anybody can do it. I had practiced it with my own parents. When human beings shipwreck themselves in an erotic ocean storm, they lose all sense of what is happening around them. They are too absorbed in that self-love which they disguise as love for someone else. Not that I'm denying that it helps to be someone like me, transparent like a piece of glass that you can't see through because it leads nowhere, which you can't use as a mirror because it reflects nobody back.

Those fragments of glass that I have for eyes enjoyed the rejection that Tristan had made of my first offer. It allowed me to establish, surreptitiously, who was in charge. If I did not feed him his quota of hints and innuendoes, he would sink back into his acquiescent rag-tag role. You treat faces, Doctor, as if they were car motors, greasing them every six months, replacing a worn-out part. You know better than anyone else that the real owner—of a car, of a face, of a person—is the one who keeps the thing going. Tristan's acquaintances had grown accustomed to him: they expected from him a certain conduct, a performance, which was dependent upon my servicing him. It wasn't long before he was back, fawning at my heels.

I have kept him by my side since then, a dog of uncertain loyalty, a dog who has grown fat on the crumbs of the data I have lavished on him.

Because even after I had acquired my camera, even after I had uselessly excavated inside the false quagmire that Enriqueta passed off as her sex, almost immediately, as soon as I left school, I realized that just as the others were graduating, in the same way it was necessary for me to change the direction of my life. And I supposed, correctly it turns out, that Tristan would accompany me wherever I went.

Up until then my activities had been carried out in the world I already knew. Easy, after all: to ransack someone who is as familiar as the scenery. Like masturbating. Not much to it. Quite another matter to dare choose a stranger, randomly, or because something in her, once in a while in him, intrigued me. That would really be splicing the umbilical cord—to comprehend that the whole world belongs to you, that there is nobody that you cannot shutter up inside your eyes.

But pleasurable as it may be to take over a face, it ends up as repetitive as the toilsome sexual rites with which so many human beings cloak their solitude. Those hands of yours, Doctor, know what I'm talking about.

Of all the features that my future victims presented to the world I extracted one above all others, like an unclean tooth inside the whitest mouth—and then what? The camera lens had stripped them—and now what? Then and now, in order to avoid boredom, it would become necessary to go beyond the mere everyday use of

somebody else's body and progress to a more profound form of pos-
session. If I could imagine an exhaustive story for that unknown face,
and if my diagnosis turned out to be true, that would be, indeed,
not only great fun and a challenge but a way of dredging the treasures from inside that person, leaving her as dry as an abandoned
mine shaft. Behind my game was the wager that anybody's inner
biography could be reconstructed by comparing her deep hidden
face with the ways in which she tried to cover and dissemble it. An
amusement that confronted me, however, with the inevitable and
final question to which I had no answer: how to find out if my
invention had any substance?

The need to find discrete, objective answers to that question has-
tened my search for the job that now, decades later, I still hold. Smile
away, Doctor. You have the right to smile. I'm using the present
tense again, and I should be speaking only of the past. The job that,
until a few days ago, until I crashed into you, I still held. That's all
right, your smile. But you must understand that gaining independence from my family was, by then, an obsession: I wanted never
again to interrupt the flow of their lives with my dimness, never
again to listen to my father outraged at a toneless voice protesting
once more that someone had put a visiting relative to sleep in my
bed, never again to watch my mother, wondering what stranger had
placed those dirty trousers and shirts in the hamper to be washed,
and then meticulously leaving them aside.

It was not easy to find the sort of work that would serve my purpose. Three conditions had to be met. The first, and most obvious,
was that I should be able to exert the only real talent I have at my
disposal, my capacity to remember any face that crosses my vision.
The second was that the job should give me access to all the available data on this city's residents, so that I could set up a network
of informers as vast as my growing photo collection. At school, my
own means had been amply sufficient, but if the whole universe was
now to be my hunting ground, I would need resources that would
be just as unlimited. A detective? A journalist? A spy? Those pro-
fessions were canceled out by the third and last of my conditions.
The work should not imperil me in any way, or bring me—it is the
same thing—any public recognition. I needed a post as burned
out and monotonous as my own face.

When I saw the ad for an apprentice to the archivist of photography files at the Department of Traffic Accidents, I knew right away that I had found what I wanted. It was satisfying also to realize that my recommendation—which amounted to an order— that Tristan Pareja study law, a career so close to power and its secrets, was beginning to bear fruit. I wasn't going to suggest that he become a plastic surgeon, now, was I, Doctor? The man had already woven a ring of law school classmates and their parents who could be influenced because of the juicy reports that I had obtained for him. Now, almost effortlessly, he managed to meet Pompeyo Garssos, the Director of the Archives, and to put in a good word for me that guaranteed me the position. Although the first few days don Pompeyo was bothered by the fact that the new employee never seemed to be at work—his eyes would slip over me, unseeing, and roam somewhere else—he soon began to appreciate my skills. Never before had that collection been as immaculately well organized: each photo easy to find, each piece of information at the tip of his fingers.

As I classified the photographs, I took a couple of seconds to look intensely at each one. A few, the more interesting ones, I would set aside; would explore the owners of those faces at my pleasure during the years to come. It was as if the whole country had become my schoolyard, allowing me to stalk an almost infinite variety of orgasms, the faces of men who beat their children and smile at their neighbors, the eyes of a woman who knows her husband is cheating but doesn't dare tell him to get out because she needs the money.

Of course, to take that initial tour of this city's adults and the countless malevolent adventures their faces promised was only the first step in a more ambitious plan, just as you, Doctor, without any doubt, gain something more than personal gratification when you alter the features of your patients.

To make headway within the Department of Traffic Accidents until I was in the exact place where I could carry out my projects, I specialized in exposing the people who had obtained fake drivers' licenses. Until I arrived at the archives, it had basically been impossible to discover if a person had filled out an application under an assumed name. Any name—which is no more than a sad jumble of sounds, at least you'll agree with me on that, Doctor—can be hidden in the great jungle of unknown names, as a tree can be hidden in a forest. You know as well as I do that the most ordinary of noses can be used to conceal the strangest face. Or am I wrong, Mardivelle? Those impostors were so sure that nobody could identify them that they didn't even take the trouble to disguise their features, they didn't even seek your help, Doctor. Later, of course, you must have made a fortune, trying to paste innocence on the most guilty faces. I could go so far as to declare that I have been at the origin of some of your most lucrative contracts. Our two careers run a parallel course—each one of us working with the counterfeit currency that shines in faces that are not ours. Attempting to make them pass the test of my eyes. Not bad at your work, Doctor. I owe you some thanks. You've made my work more entertaining. More challenging.

But at the time it was as easy as can be. Before the other employees arrived, very early in the morning, I would select from the multitude of applications that had been signed the previous day, the ones harboring suspicious features. I would recognize that the name was false right away, just as I realized that Patricia was lying about her own name as soon as I saw her face. Then I would let my memory loose in the enormous pit of photographs that shimmered in the nearby files, and I would, a few moments later, go straight to the original face and pick it out. Hours later, each fraudulent application for a driver's license would find itself on top of Pompeyo Garssos's desk, next to another photograph of the same person, taken from the archives, but with the real name attached.

Just as I had with Tristan, I preferred letting someone else lap up all the credit: rather soon, the Director of the Archives had begun to acquire a legendary reputation for detecting false I.D.s. As for me, I got the only thing I wanted: to be his secretary.

Of course I didn't solve all the deceptive cases that came my way. It was indispensable to leave some in doubt, even if I already knew whom to look for, all the details of yet another sham life. Otherwise, what pretext could I use to start demanding data from other agencies and institutions, both public and private? Supposedly to check up on the delinquents, but in fact to establish my own network. I would ask, let's say, the Drug Bureau for an inquiry on someone. I would then set up an initial contact with an agent at the Bureau; he would be offered a service, a tidbit of news, a confidential report, and that is the way, slowly and smoothly as ever, I would have him ready to work for me.

It would be quite dull, Doctor, and even makes me want to yawn myself, to give you details about how I lured each puny informant into my web. Apply the Tristan Pareja model, with slight variations, and you can guess how it all happened. One source in each neuralgic information center—the Police Computer, the Insurance Agents' Data Base, the Universal Health Care Office, the Division of Bank Accounts, the Credit Watchers' Union, the Drug Bureau, the assistant to the assistant librarian at the most important newspaper in the country—no need for more than one person. Somebody who, without my intervention, would be less than nothing. Armed with the reports smuggled to me by the others, I snarled and tied up each one of them, I sugared their ambition and promised them power that their mediocre minds had not dared to envision. I let them crest on a steady wave of information until they were, each of them in their respective places, bound for glory, solving impossible enigmas, revealing the answers to cases that had been closed for years, detecting criminals with the facility of housewives identifying the rotten apple in the barrel. They became addicts of the celebrity I gave them. They could not escape from me.

Until you called them on the phone, Doctor, until you destroyed what I thought were impregnable defenses.

But you still have no idea who I am, Doctor. Because I destroyed every last file that contained a reference to my existence. I had been born as if dead. I would live as if dead, without leaving so much as a fingerprint on the world's surface.

The subjects chosen by my camera had left many prints, on the other hand, any number of school grades and medical reports; and with this and so much more it was easy to discover their whole itinerary. I could at least find out if the image I had captured corresponded at all to the story I had invented for them. I was on target, in general, Doctor, and getting better as time went on: each new expedition, each new darkened flash, brought me closer to perfection. And what is more, the taking of the photos themselves became an easier task.

Each human being has around him a hive of almost infinite relationships, people stuck to his life as if it were flypaper, people mixed into his jam, his clothing, his checkbook, his toilet paper. The things people have been told that they need to live, the things somebody else always has to furnish. So that once my victim's face appeared—on the street, in the paper, lost and twisted, lightning-like, in a crowd filmed by a TV crew—and once I had followed that face into the bowels of my endless files, where her name and address were always awaiting me, the next step was to locate the men and women who surrounded and serviced her. If you can get those people to cooperate, the perfect irreplaceable snapshot is not only within reach. It is as easy as spitting.

I had the telephone repairman, with direct access to such and such an apartment—I had that man at my beck and call. Not because of a photo I had taken of him. I wasn't going to run around snapping everybody, the vilest and least interesting people who crawl this earth—just as you, Doctor, would not dream of operating on a blind beggar. To do so would have exhausted our energies quite quickly. Just a couple of brief reports on him, his police record, his bank account, his kid's school grades, his mother's medical ups and downs—enough to enlist him in a supporting role for my assault. Each person, no matter how insignificant he may seem, has the key to some door—and it is by opening doors, Mirvallori, that you take photographs. You're an expert at closing doors and closing faces, excluding others from your operating room so nobody can tell how you play the piano of each face, how you recompose the obscure music of each face. I know your statements and I know your habits, Doctor. For me, on the other hand, doors are like water, Doctor. The mailmen, the maids and the help, the dry cleaner, delivery boy, janitor, the old schoolmarm: all of them, keys to some kind of lock. Keys that do not know my fingers turning them, keys that do not remember my features.

How were they to retain me in their memory if not even my closest contacts, not even my parents, were able to do that? After fattening those agents for years, after having been the only architect of their fortunes—and I followed them because it was their turn, as well, to be photographed by me—would you believe that they did not realize I was present, as if I were a total stranger? I'll admit it, this ended up bothering me: it came to a point where, finally, if I needed some message from them that they could not entrust to the phone or the mail, rather than go myself I would send Tristan Pareja to pick it up.

They have been so dependent on me these years that it has been difficult for me to conceive of their betrayal. I've seen it more as an act of suicide on their part than as an act of aggression against me. The fact that someone now knew their identity and had been insinuating terrible things about the hollow of my face, insinuations that were all the more terrible because they may have approached the truth of what I was, that fact did not overly alarm me. I thought that Monday I would rein them in. As soon as I could investigate you, Mavirelli, slip into your home one night or wide-angle you from a corner of your operating room at the very moment when you began to intervene inside someone else's body, as soon as I had you in my little machine, Doctor, as soon as I had pierced your power as if it were a suppuration, stripping your mask from you with the same brutality with which you press it down upon others. That would be enough, I thought—and I still think so, Doctor—to transform myself once more into the magnet for those poor floating fragments of nothingness. Then they would come in supplication, as Tristan Pareja had come into the schoolyard some weeks after he had indignantly rejected my proposal that he sell the news I was giving him. And if not them, then others—because that network was entirely replaceable by any other. I had lifted them up from an anonymous sewer, and if I felt like it, that is where they would return, drop by drop.

Or at least that is what I thought until I saw Tristan Pareja's face in my living room. Only at that moment, when I came down the stairs, leaving Oriana's wonders—and what wonders they are, Doctor—only then did I understand that my situation was much more exposed than I had believed it to be.

I did not steer Tristan to the bar because I ever imagined that I personally would need a lawyer someday. So public an occurrence as a lawsuit was practically inconceivable. What I wanted was someone who could glide his way through the pores of society just as you, Doctor, slime your way through the skin of your patients, just like that. But when I returned home that night of the

accident, Marverelhi, and after the phone rang and your unidenti-
fiable underling hung up on me, the first person I tried to contact
was Tristan Pareja.

I was adamant about getting you declared guilty at the Police
Court this coming Wednesday, Doctor. It would have been prudent
to accept that I had made a mistake, that this disobedient foot of
mine had pushed down on the accelerator instead of on the brake;
and if you had been anybody else, that's how things would have
ended up. Let the insurance take care of the damages, hush up any
complications with a couple of phone calls. That there might have
been some minor scandal weighed on me—a newspaper headline
(which, strangely enough, you have not planted anywhere, Doctor)
screaming about officials of the Department of Traffic Accidents
so flagrantly ignoring the signals. But nothing that we couldn't
fix like gentlemen.

What moved me was something else. You didn't have to be a
mastermind—and if there is one thing I can do, it is to read situa-
tions as gypsies read the future in cards—to realize that you were
in an uncomfortable predicament: rushing your lover to her home
before having to run back to your own place, on Christmas Eve,
no less. Not a good time to have an accident, Doctor. And if you
did not know me, Marvirelli, I had no trouble recognizing you.
Even if you did not owe me for Alicia's absence, even if you had
not been provoking me all these years with your front-cover interviews in glossy magazines, I had already noted you down for some
weekend, some vacation, when I could take the time to work on a
particularly intricate case. Just as others look forward to visiting a
city full of museums or theaters, that's how I had kept you, Doctor,
in the back of my mind, like a succulent dessert that one always
saves for the end. If I had not yet indulged myself, it may have been
because something inside warned me that you were no ordinary
adversary, that you were more dangerous, and that I should drink
you up and down only at the right moment.

So if it had been anybody else, I'd have acted with my normal
caution. Win the big battles, never lose a minute or waste an effort
on marginal issues. But it was my desire, Doctor, to impose myself
upon you ignominiously, to defeat you barefacedly—if you are not
annoyed by the wordplay.

With a strange woman in your car and no Alicia in mine, you were in a losing position. For once, someone else was going to wreak upon you a face that was not yours. And that person was none other than this nonentity who is speaking to you right now from afar. Let the bastard pay the damages, I thought to myself. As if I was asking you to endorse a check. Money scratched from each face that you had approached with your scalpel, the white light glowing behind you; it was like expropriating your cosmetics, as if you had been working as my menial all these years. The final act of the patient acts of sabotage I had been carrying out. First, Moronevi, I had been fingering your patients day in and day out, no matter what you did with them, no matter the about-faces, the silicone cheek implants, the thickened, sticky lips, the disappearing crow's-feet, the metastasis of the nostrils, the shifted teeth, the tightening of the skull bones, the foreshortening of the hairline. Each face you recomposed, I returned to its original in the laboratory that seethed in my head. That was first. Next, I messed up your car and, along the way, your reputation. And third. Third: you pay me with the dividends debauched from faces that never belonged to you.

Understand, Doctor: it was a way of kicking your mug in, a way of stripping you naked in public, a way of showing who owns this city, you who disguise people or I who open the shutters of their pretense. And I would do this, besides, without recourse to photography: to defeat someone that powerful, to make him concede my existence in the world without having to use my camera. It is proof of your strength, Doctor, that I ended up taking a picture of you.

The first case, at any rate, for Tristan Pareja.

I started to call him from the police precinct where both of us had been taken so as to stamp our contradictory statements. When I saw that you, Marcarelsohn, were closely watching me dial, your eyes flashing with mistrust, as if you doubted that someone so patently vulgar and second-rate could have any sort of important friend, I hung up before speaking. But I fell into the trap that vanity once in a while opens for us. Perhaps for the first time in my life I wanted to impress someone with something as discardable and superficial as an influential contact. I bragged about my relationship with Pareja, that famous lawyer, so that you, Doctor, would spend a whole night thinking you had crashed with a dangerous adversary. Now I know that you spent the night thinking about other things.

But it didn't seem suspicious, when, upon returning home, Pareja's phone was busy and stayed that way for the next few hours. I was worn out with the pain and the excitement, and I lay down, unhooked the receiver so the hidden caller wouldn't awaken me, and fell asleep. When I managed to get hold of Tristan the next day, he insisted there was nothing to worry about. It was enough that I obtain three witnesses who swore that I was telling the truth. They would be pitted against the equally fraudulent witnesses, three of them, that Doctor Mavirelli was going to introduce (Pareja made no mistake while pronouncing your name, Doctor)—and we would win hands down, because it was then that we would threaten our enemy with revealing the presence of his lover that night of the crash. I assigned no importance to the fact that Pareja did not rush over immediately, that same day. It was Christmas, after all, when everybody, except for you-know-who, spends the day with their family.

Nor did it seem difficult, even in my limping condition, to secure the three witnesses. Each one of my contacts could get me ten times that number. But when a whole day of busy telephones passed, when my contacts systematically one after the other refused to talk to me, it was then, on Friday morning, precisely one hour before Patricia returned with such insolence to ring my bell, that I decided to call Tristan Pareja again and tell him to drop in as soon as possible. A quick visit by him to the homes of my contacts, an allusion to their children's vulnerability, the mention of a secret that they thought was well concealed, any one of these would rapidly reduce them to what they essentially were: my captives.

I insist I was not alarmed. I understood that the same henchman of yours who was calling me was calling them, as well; it was almost with joy—if you would allow someone like me the use of such a word—that I guessed your role in the affair, your panic: each telephone that did not answer was a genuflection that you made in my direction, Doctor. For the first time somebody was accepting me as a gigantic rival, worthy of the battle which, unfortunately for you, I am about to win.

Although when I saw Tristan, the first doubts arose in my mind.
Perhaps because I knew instantly—I knew it in images, I knew it,
one photo after another announcing what had happened in his house,
which might be far from my gaze but was so near my imagination—
that he had betrayed me. His phone had been busy because you,
or your subservant, Doctor, were talking to him, you were the one
who was acquiring his list of my assistants, you were the one who
was joining them in a parallel circuit from which I, like a tumor in
the brain, could be eliminated. Busy because perhaps there was no
hireling at all and it was the selfsame Pareja who had been calling
each of them with the message that it was to their advantage to deny
me. Busy because he was taking over my network for his own benefit
or even—he has always been such a coward, this Pareja—for your
exclusive use, Doctor. Busy because if he joined them into a group
outside my controlling center, I would no longer be indispensable
to them, to him, or to any of the other disparate contacts I had so
laboriously sought out. Busy because I myself had given them too
much power, allowing them to grow refractory and independent.
Busy, finally, because it might well have been Pareja himself who
dialed my number in order to hang up after mocking me with a
chuckle, leaving me with that sterile receiver in my hand.

And if I was in want of any more proof of his villainy and of
my lack of further ascendancy in his life, he gave it to me without
blinking an eyelash. Tristan Pareja did not recognize me.

"I was looking for—" he said, as if looking at me through a haze,
and added my name, glancing around everywhere, as if I might be
hidden behind some piece of furniture rather than standing there
directly in view of the insolent laziness of his eyes. Tristan was apt
to remember me better than most other human beings: after all, his
prestige, his career, depended on it. Which did not mean that we
did not have misencounters, especially in public places, where he
could remain at my side, without seeing me, for hours. But never
had such clumsiness surfaced at a place where he expected to find
me, and certainly never in my own dwelling. Patricia remembered
me more clearly than he did. Not to mention Alicia. There was no
doubt: his memory of me was growing pale. He no longer knew
who I was, no longer recalled the lackluster color of my hair, these
dull, blurred eyes of mine.

The fact that he could not salvage my face from the thousands of faces withering in his mind caused me no indignation. On the contrary, it may have been precisely that forgetfulness which bathed me in a strange tranquility. I had always contemplated the eventuality that I would part ways with Pareja: there was no reason, considering, why he should demonstrate toward me affection or loyalty or any other of those cunning attitudes that humans swear will be eternal and that last only so long as convenience demands. We were—we had been—partners because it was suitable to us both. It was now advantageous for him to seek refuge under the wing of a plastic surgeon who had sculpted and sewn up the most pre-eminent faces in the country, the public faces with which the powerful governed, the looks that the history books would gather for the admiration of future generations. But his blindness toward me, along with my absolute certainty that I could still read his every wrinkle, indicated to me at the same time that I was as much the master of my own destiny as I had been that fatal day when I had collected the scraps of those smelly photos and had realized what extraordinary predaceousness over others they might afford me. If I felt like it, I could follow him with my camera without his perceiving me—there was nothing to stop me from sending the most outrageous snapshots to all his clients; from letting his lovely wife examine the evidence of his encounters with animals; from sending to the school principal the image of his son shoplifting at the local drugstore. And I would keep for myself, Doctor Marcavelli, the instant photo in which he met with you. I would frame it over my bed as a reminder that we should never let a quarry go once we have it cooking over our fire.

But I would do none of these.

I quite simply let Tristan Pareja depart from my life by telling him that the gentleman whom he wished to speak with was not there for the moment. Later on I would call him to spread the lie that I had already obtained the three witnesses and that we should get together the afternoon of the court appearance to plan our strategy. I cannot say if I had decided by then not even to go. What is certain is that I had not yet realized it was time to seek an appointment with you, Mirvarelli. There was so much still to live through before that: I had to visit former Inspector Jarvik; I had to understand that the only way of keeping Oriana and protecting her was to journey abroad. I still did not know who Oriana was. But the hypocrisy that had taken over Pareja's face confirmed the ruin you were planning for me. I knew that there was no longer anybody in the world who could front for me, and the idea that it might be imperative for both of us to meet without intermediaries, that distant idea, began to dawn in my eyes.

My helper for thirty years moved away from me without the slightest sign that he had recognized me.

It was the last time I saw him in my life.

Was I under the innocent influence of Oriana? Was that why I did not even think of an act of vengeance? Was it her sweet infancy that had produced this calm?

Oriana was upstairs, Oriana who was a clean photograph of her own soul. Sitting on my bed, waiting obediently for me to mount up to her, not budging her body, her shoeless feet rhythmically swaying back and forth. Oriana upstairs, with nothing to hide. Oriana, waiting for me.

And so are you, Doctor. You, as well. Soon. But Oriana comes first.

H ave you noticed, Doctor, the importance human beings attach to the act of baring themselves? As if to undress were a symbol of their vow not to cheat the other person, the man, the woman, who is watching, the symbol of the vow to display themselves without the shield of their previous lives, naked as if they had just been born. But as you know and your pockets full of money know, Doctor, those unclothed bodies never divest themselves of their face. They may swear the most eternal of devotions, but the truth is that they spend the rest of their short lives probing their lover's eyes, wanting and not wanting to guess the coming betrayal. Trying to make believe that there is no shadow of a plastic surgeon falling between each man and each woman.

Oriana was once that sort of person. I have no doubt that somewhere in this city there are people who dispose of a report—which you shall get for me, have no doubt about it— where the falseness of what used to be her adult life is written out; a life as full of recesses and duplicity as that of any other human being. It is my luck that she does not remember that life. Oriana is the first woman I have ever met, Doctor, whom I do not need to photograph. The first in which the photo would reveal less than what she already has written all over the fullness of her face.

So I found myself uncovering the only thing that was left to be uncovered: that body, mature and sensual and feminine. I lay her bare slowly, with an almost tropical rhythm, a question about her past falling and an answer that she did not know falling with every garment, and then both of us murmuring that it did not matter if she, if I, if we, had no knowledge whatever about who she had

once been, because we were going to enter the realm of who she
was now. As if we had all the time in the world. Except that I, for
one, do not have all the time in the world, Doctor. With the other
women, yes, obviously, I did. From the moment that the camera
was mine, they were all within reach, for as long as I liked. It was
all the same if I captured them now or later: they would be no less
dishonest with themselves tomorrow than today. It was all the
same if they disappeared: they were infinitely replaceable by other
images just as intoxicating. It was all the same if today the door to
the shower was closed: the day after tomorrow, having found the
subordinate who could usher me in, having discovered the right
piece of information, having cornered the plumber, my lens would
be waiting for her behind the bushes or near her bed.

Oriana is different. I saw her in front of me, transparent and
enigmatic and entirely disrobed of all protection, whether in words
or in clothes, and I wondered—never had I asked such a question,
I do not even have a name to give to this fear that shrieks inside
me—if she were going to escape. It was not a physical evasion that
I feared, Doctor. Nobody— not even someone like you, Doctor,
as you shall discover in a few hours' time—can run from my eyes.
But Oriana might— and here the pain in my thoughts trickled into
what must have been my heart; she might—and this could be happening right at this moment, as I speak to you; Oriana might break
away from her own self, awaken from her amnesia, and become
again the ordinary everyday person she once was, in other words,
precisely one of those beings without a mystery to hide who bore
me to death, the kind that visit you, Doctor, so you can continue
to perpetrate your repertory of faces upon them.

When I used to make love with those women, Doctor, I never
got to the bottom of them. It is possible that they may have had,
deep within their selves, perhaps, an image of the Paradise that
they had lost, of a time in which they were not the window dressing that others had forced them to become in order to exist. Too
deep to find it: their childhood. I was never able to descend to that
zone, if it was there, inside them. It was necessary to beat open
a track through a whole garbage jungle of honey-dipped-beige
natural-blush coloring creams, everything that revolts me, the eternal scripts and jingles, the body lotion and the body sales and the

body cleansers and the body tonics, all the rose refining masks and the nonoily skin supplements—layer upon layer of make-up and memories which each person uses to induce the other to love him or her, to convince the other that this partner is a good investment. One face after the other that I classify inside my own filing system so that they will never have a chance to manipulate me, just as the police keep and study a rogues' gallery of the worst criminals, just as children rehearse and perfect one face after the other for the audience that starts to disrobe them as of a certain age, just as they learn the gestures with which they will have to become the managers of themselves from a certain age onward.

An age that Oriana has not yet reached.

I had to entrust myself to my sex so that it would help me discover what up till then more perceptive organs had only muttered to me. Abandoned by my camera, unable to explore through my eyes the eclipse of Oriana's unknown face, I could only begin to explore the identity of this twin of mine by entering her supposedly alien body and making it my own, pressing the crushed grapes in my fingers to feel what she was feeling, I with no face and she with no past, the two mirrors reflecting nothing more than each the other and the other again. Because if somebody or something has erased, as if it had never existed, her whole life after she was five, nobody has been able, on the other hand, to banish the experience of those years from her body. She may talk like a small girl, but she makes love like an adult woman.

And that's why I'm in a hurry, Doctor. That's why I need to procure her secret file.

You think it's because I'm scared? That those men who are searching for her have me on the run?

Let them look for her all they want, let them wear out the soles of their shoes shuffling up and down the whole country. By tomorrow night we'll be abroad—thanks to you, Doctor. Yes. You may not know it yet, but you're going to give us everything we need.

My haste has other origins.

Oriana's previous existence is not registered in that report alone. Her true history is also known by some adult Oriana who is crouched within that child Oriana who stretched out her arms to me so that I could protect her. That older woman is determined to come back to the surface and transform my loved one into a normal, orthodox, uninteresting being, one of those millions that stroll along the streets with their jeans pressed so closely to their buttocks that you might presume they had a secret to conceal and didn't want it to come out. Pretending they have some sort of real enigma in there, between their skin and their clothing, something that might be worth exploring. Normal: someone with a past, with a mask, with a piece of lipstick. A person like you, Doctor, like Enriqueta, like Tristan Pareja.

I am going to prevail against her.

My sex suggests to me that she is in there, preparing her revenge, watching the almost-five-year-old Oriana from a corner in her brain, from a curtain, from the corrupt camera of a pair of concealed eyes in there. Watching me as I listen to her Evelike mewls of pleasure, watching us make love, lying next to us in bed, lying on her back when Oriana gets on top of me, planning the merciless day when she will again take by assault the face that once belonged to her.

I will not allow her to interpose her memories between us.

It is a decision I made Saturday at dawn, the first morning that we shared. That was when Oriana's hand awoke my shoulder, and the lips of Oriana in my hair and Oriana's body in the sheets, and she asked me something that I myself, with all my prophetic inclinations, would have been unable to predict:

"Hey, who are you?"

And as I was in no condition to answer, she said, "I'm almost five years old," with that shine in her eyes that indicates that there is no double-dealing in her of any sort. "You can call me Oriana. I think that's my name."

And then, as I was still stupefied, still silent:

"Will you take care of me? 'Cause there are some men who are looking for me . . . Somebody told me that I had to hide."

So this woman, Doctor, not only has stopped growing in order to remain forever on the threshold of her five years of age, not only does not retain in her memory her real name, who her parents might be, and where she was born, but does not remember what just happened to her yesterday. For once, I didn't mind if somebody didn't recognize me: she treats everybody the same way. Nobody has a permanent face in her world, a world where someone like me can compete, can triumph. Her eyes went blank when I mentioned Patricia's name, when I asked her about the games we had played the preceding night.

Sunday morning was a repeat performance of Saturday. Except that I was the one who woke her this time, anxious to find out if the miracle would continue, and once more, "Hey, who are you?" and again the same voice introducing itself as if we had not already spent two long days of loving together, "I think my name may be Oriana," and again, "What are we going to play today?" and "Watch out, there are some men who are—" and then I knew, I knew that if we were to stay together, it was absolutely essential to destroy any chance that the woman who had once occupied that body should come to disturb us.

I am going to keep her forever, Doctor.

Because if I had to present myself to her all over again on Saturday and Sunday and yesterday and today, her fingers, conversely, still knew me, her skin had not forgotten my touch. In her hands and in the permanent sanctuary that she offered me, there remained the wisdom from the days we had lived; and there, as well, shall be deposited the different identities that I will bestow upon her.

I need nothing more in the universe: Oriana, because of her unanchored memory, that double amnesia of hers, Maravelli, is a perpetual adventure. That she should not have the slightest idea of who she is, that she has even lost the previous day's experience, lets me choose for her, upon our awakening, an original role. I don't expect this to shock you too much, Doctor. You do the same thing. You select the face for each patient—and if you don't like it, you change it. I also select a face; but mine, unlike yours, lasts only twenty-four hours. That Saturday, for instance, not knowing if the next day she would forget again, I told Oriana that her real name was Enriqueta and filled her in on the life of the girl who had twisted my destiny with her doll and my drawings. I had always wanted to possess Enriqueta—not through a photograph, not through the unfaithful steward of my sex, but to have her under my sway the way a character belongs to an author, to be able to give that story between us, if I so desired, an ending that supplied more satisfaction, to be able to relive once and again that scene in the playhouse in her garden until it came out exactly as I had dreamt it, so that the victim was Enriqueta and not me. Monday, yesterday morning, in fact, I let her play Alicia, and Alicia did not submit to you, Doctor. She stepped away from your office door and accepted me rather than the face which you had prepared for her.

Of course I will not select Enriqueta or Alicia each time. At the beginning of the day, and today indeed that is what I did, I can offer to Oriana one of those women who are in my files, one I have followed and explored, or tomorrow a woman I have invented from one of the thousand photographs I chanced upon in the archives, or the day after tomorrow one of the women I have read about who died thousands of years ago: a saint, a queen, a heretic, a witch, a whore, a movie star. She can be real, she can be fictional: the only circumstance that never changes is that she always ends up at my mercy, always ends up awaiting my indulgence, my forgiveness.

She disguises herself and we play until the sun goes down.

The last five days of my life, Doctor, have therefore been played out as a drama whose basic direction I have written ahead of time but whose variations and developments will be improvised by the two actors, a drama where I invariably control the final act of coupling. She doesn't want to invent her own role. She couldn't if she wanted to. With no memories to orient her, she is grateful that somebody else should guide her existence, she thanks me simply for not scolding her or leaving her locked up in a room.

Boring? For me?

Why, aren't you bored by the same woman every day or by so many women who are all the same, all of them believing in the role written for them by some demon of their unhappiness inside their head, written by their P.R. agent inside, written by their need to please some man? Whereas Oriana knows that this pastime is provisional and fleeting, no matter how passionately she may practice it: at the end of the entertainment I will be waiting to return to her the gift of her childhood. Other women should envy her: who would not want to live the most perverse of aberrations, to descend to the sewers of the human soul, and emerge without a scratch, without having to ask questions or tremble in fear, able to awaken the next day soothed by forgetfulness, ready for yet another voyage of discovery?

Why should she feel unfortunate? For her, every day shall be as a first birth, with all the fresh air that came at the beginning of Creation. And the person who accompanies her, the person who can show her the perpetually recent contours of the universe, will be as a god.

Doctor, I had no childhood. I grew old all at once. My eyes forced the rest of my body to hurry. Now, with Oriana's eternal fountain flowing through my life, I am becoming young again: it has been merely a matter of seeing the world with the fertility of those eyes of hers that dawn with such clarity each morning; it has been a matter of recreating each day from her nothingness a new personality. She is as Eve. But I shall not be Adam, I shall be God and the Serpent rolled up into one, starting the day as God and ending it as the Serpent, with the chance to begin the next day another story, a new galaxy, another Garden and another Exile, until the end of time. I can rewrite and recapture the whole of human history. We can be each of the past's lovers, each character in each novel: and it will always be my narrating her, a thousand and one times if that is necessary.

How glad I would have been, that Sunday, to have scoured her forever, to have explored her transitory day-being and that more permanent nocturnal self inside, her one day-mind and her forever-body. But that urgency in me, Doctor, that fear that she might disappear from under my hands at the next moment . . . I have been a watcher for too long not to know that inside each cell there is a voyeur, in each stump of her blood, that other Oriana was watching me through the keyhole eyes of all my own Orianas, the hard holes of those pretty eyes that I have now claimed, preparing herself to come out and take from me that childhood that I was always denied.

It was that sense of urgency, that haste to kidnap her for all time, the fear that time was running out, the cloudy photograph forming in my mind of someone inside who is searching for her, somebody's hand caressing a report on her; that was what drove me to go to the office that day. I still did not know, that same Sunday morning when I decided to keep her forever, that I would eventually turn to you, Doctor. I thought that my files would be more than sufficient to accomplish my purposes, to find the minimal

information on Oriana's identity, the data that would allow me to
reactivate my network.

But let me make one thing clear. If I finally decided to obtain
some sort of intelligence on the woman Oriana had once been, it
was as a preventive measure, not as a road toward her true being.
Who knows better than I that those mediocre reports are of no con-
sequence compared to the fierce probe of one of my photographs?
I concluded that it was important to use this imperfect substitute
to explore Oriana's past, because I have no other way of reading
what she once was, because I have no other way of protecting her
from the ghost she carries inside. I needed clues, I thought, however inconsiderable, to understand the outlines of her previous existence and to sketch out the references I must drastically elude in
the future. I have read that some casual allusion to a past incident
could restore her memory, restore her to the rattrap from which
she had enabled herself to escape. This was my way of assuring her
an unperturbed and blissful captivity.

What I did not expect, on the other hand, was that my key would
not fit into the lock on the back door of the Transportation Min-
istry. Someone had changed it. I tried to go in through the front
door. It was barred. Naturally, when the porter arrived, sleepy and
ill-tempered, he didn't recognize me. I showed him my identity
pass. He looked at the name and then, with all brazenness, he put
it away in one of his pockets.

"That's right," he said, yawning. "They told me you'd be coming
by. I've got a signed order—from Pompeyo Garssos. Here it is: you
don't work here, anymore."

I did not bother to discuss the matter with him.

If this had happened to me a week before, it would have had no
effect upon me. It would merely have been a matter of returning
there in another hour. The idiot would not remember me, and I
would easily persuade him to let me in under another name. Or if
that didn't work, the very next day, a Monday, I could pass under his
blind and bleary eyes, mixed in with the crowd of other employees.
Once inside, I could slip among the papers like a phantom, gathering Oriana's data and the other reports I needed to reconstruct my
empire without anybody so much as realizing I was there.

I had always done things slowly. Prudence suggested it. So did principle. But what I was lacking now was time, Doctor, time, which had always been my main ally.

I saw your hand in all this immediately, the message you were sending me. That I should go to see you, that we should work this matter out like men. You had stolen my tranquility, you had destroyed my network, now you were taking my job. And who knows what other surprises you had in store, Doctor—in my office, on the street, at home.

So you have only yourself to blame for having attracted me to your private operating room. It was all the same to me by then, Doctor, if I ended your career as a face peddler or if I let you go scot-free. The only thing I cared about was to save the woman who had the only face in this world that was not for sale. Behind me, as if the sound itself accentuated my own decision, I heard the porter shut the gate with a double lock, disappearing into the bowels of the building that for so many years had been the temple of all my knowledge and the headquarters for all my contacts. I did not allow myself even a smudge of nostalgia for its loss.

As it is you, Doctor, who are denying me the use of what it has taken me a whole lifetime to construct, it seems fair to me that it should therefore be you who will submit to me the resources with which I intend to solve my problems.

If I did not want to continue finding obstacles in my path, the time had come to confront you directly, Doctor, to ask for an appointment.

But with your permission, Mierdavelli, first I'll take your photograph.

I want you to fix your eyes on this snapshot. Do you recognize anybody? Do you recognize the person who is operating? Looks like you, doesn't it, Doctor? Or are you going to deny, do you dare to deny, what your hands are doing? You don't? Another question, then. Would you like that patient, the woman you operated on that day, to receive a copy? Or should I send it to her husband, Colonel Zagasto? Or would you rather that the photo be sent to one of the thousands of other city residents whose faces you have been purging all these years—without the inquisitive presence of my camera? Yes, Doctor. I also have a list of your patients.

How did I do all this?

You are forewarned: I could have done it on my own. It is true that I no longer have my files. True that you have dispersed my contacts. And true also that my errand boy, Tristan, is now at somebody else's insidious beck and call. But even so, Malavierro, your fortress is not inaccessible. Anyone persistent, ready to be rendered invisible by holding his breath, could have negotiated an entry into the hospital where you usually operate, could have crossed the eight additional security checks, mounted the staircase that leads to your private chambers, neutralized the infrared alarm rays. Anyone could have witnessed from one of the dark walls the ceremonies that I witnessed that day. Just so you know: if tomorrow I do not have Oriana by my side like a living howl, tomorrow if I feel like it, tomorrow I can once again smuggle myself, this time without anyone's aid, into your operating room.

So you won't misconstrue the fact that I asked for that aid, so you'll believe that on that Sunday when I left my office, I hadn't even thought of it, so you'll know that what was burning up my eyes was that dossier of Oriana's and nothing else. It was not fear that drove me to turn to the one person who was not on the list that Tristan Pareja had slipped into your hands, the one person you couldn't use against me, the last secret contact that I never mentioned to anybody: former Inspector Federico Jarvik. That's not what he's called, of course—but most of the names that I mention here are not the real ones, except for the name you inherited from the fornicators who produced you, Mavarello, and I keep confusing that one.

Why should I make your task easy? Haven't you declared in interviews that names are no more than "a muddled and precarious mixture of syllables," whereas the face is eternal? Haven't you said that? Haven't you said that even the face of someone who was born with the most undistinguished features in the world, that even that face you could transform into something wonderful? If what you say is true, then you should be able, as I am, to identify every person immediately without needing to know what sad, fragile sounds their parents gave to them—like branding cattle, Doctor—at birth.

Because it was that talent which brought to me one day precisely the stone-faced man with the impenetrable eyes whom I have baptized with the name of Federico Jarvik. He didn't come to talk to you, Doctor. He came to talk to me.

He strode directly into the small office I had next to Pompeyo Garssos's vast chambers and sat down in front of me. He remained there for a couple of seconds without saying a word, looking at me parsimoniously, as if he were trying to fix me in his memory and it were costing him no end of trouble.

"Jarvik," he stated finally. "Bureau of Investigations." And then, almost at once, "Why should I show you my I.D.? You have ways of knowing that I'm telling the truth. I'll meet you at the corner coffee shop. I don't want to talk here."

I wondered whether to accept his invitation. Not because I was afraid that the police might be onto my photographic adventures, although I'll admit to the faintest hint of disquiet about that. All human beings feel revulsion when they watch their enemies eating, isn't that so, Doctor? But I don't know one who had to look on, as I did, while members of his family devoured the food in front of his hungry eyes. Naturally I could steal from one plate or another and concoct a supper of odds and ends. It's only that those mouths hypnotized me: it was as if they were chewing me, transferring energy from my body so they could grow more and eat more each day. At times hatred stuns you, Doctor. I would awaken from my daze and all the plates would be empty already, and my parents and brothers and sisters would be getting up from the table and there was not a scrap left to purloin. Their faces like those dirty plates. The tongues licking the lips as sweepers wash from a city street the hairs of a dog which has just been squashed by a drunken truck. Have you never seen the way in which people salivate before a meal, have you never forced yourself to imagine the descent into the secret cesspools of the body, where neither you nor anyone else has ever gone? How can you, after that, break bread in somebody's company? For me it was much better not to sit down at the table. Not that one. Not any other one. Ever again. From the moment I decided to pick among the dregs of their food, pass the mire that they left behind through the sieve of my eyes, I never again sat down at my enemies' table. I can assure you they did not miss me.

Fortunately the impassive and prim lips of the inspector were sipping only a cup of coffee. When I approached the table, without taking a seat, he hesitated, as if he thought I might be the waiter bringing him a glass of water. But I realized that he had, after all, managed to recognize me.

"It's taken me years to find you," he said, after I rejected his offer of refreshment. "I am now able to comprehend why it was so complicated."

I answered that I did not know what he was referring to and that if he wished to speak to the director, today was not the best day to—

"I came to meet you," he interrupted. "You're responsible for all the cases that have been solved, the ones that take care of the false I.D.s, aren't you? And don't make me lose valuable time telling me it's Pompeyo, because my observations and statistics prove that he never fingered a false license before you arrived, and that if you leave, he'll never finger another one."

A more vulnerable person would have felt alarmed at what seemed like the end of anonymity. But it would not be necessary to change employment, alter my name again, surreptitiously build another network. My gaze had already infiltrated the defenses that surrounded that young inspector's face. His implacability was no more than a façade. My zoom could, any evening, discover the buttons that had to be undone in order to domesticate him.

It turned out, however, that the definitive photo, which I snapped of him a couple of weeks later, was never required. The inspector treated me with no hostility. As if he respected me. He had no intention, he said, of disturbing the privacy that I quite evidently cherished to such a degree. If I did not wish to use my rather uncommon skills to their fullest in some superior position, he was not one to dispute my choice. And if there was anything that he could do in order to facilitate the sort of inquiries in which, or so it seemed, I was immersed . . . But he had, if I did not mind, some favors to ask me. It was confidential work, so much so that he preferred not to make the request through official channels. He did not think that the Director of the Archives should be involved. Moreover, I should tell no one that I had been contacted. That was why, from now on, we would always meet outside the office: at this coffee shop, at his house, or at mine if I authorized such an invasion of my own space.

The services the inspector demanded of me were of two sorts. The first was not so different from what I had already been doing: he would give me certain photos, I would discover their real identity in my files. The second service posed a more challenging task: if he were to describe a face to me, rich in detail, would I be able to pinpoint, among the millions of photos in the archives, the corresponding person?

And if I did not cooperate?

"You'll cooperate," Jarvik said. "It's easier than running."

He was right. Now that he had hunted me down, he wouldn't leave me alone—not a detective as tenacious as he had proved to be. He had figured out my skill for remembering faces, though he did not seem to suspect what I did with my camera. If I just disappeared and resurfaced at another, similar post, he would trace me to my new hideaway after a couple of years, maybe months, and then he wouldn't be as easygoing with me as he now was. It was better to have him as an ally. I didn't care, after all, what he did with the faces and data I'd bestow upon him. I even said to myself—so you can see, Doctor, that something in the desultory ice of my eyes already anticipated Pareja's betrayal—that it might be good to establish some independent contact to whom I could turn in case my network broke down. It was only years later that I realized that it was also to Jarvik's advantage to keep our collaboration in the shadows. When the government changed and they kicked him out of the bureau or he resigned or something of the sort—I have never been interested in politics, Doctor—he let me know that he intended to continue as a private investigator and that he saw no reason to end a relationship that had been so fruitful. If I wanted to continue assisting him, he still had excellent contacts inside the police and everywhere else, and he hoped that someday he would find a way of compensating me for my services.

I had never needed any such compensation. Up until now. At last, after years of granting him favors, it was my turn to ask him for one. Unless you, Doctor, or Pareja or another of your cronies had gotten in touch with him before I had.

But Jarvik had escaped you, Doctor. I knew it as soon as he opened the door to his apartment and he was able, with the usual strenuous effort, his eyes wrinkling up, his face frozen into its habitual mask, to identify me. And what is more, he still needed me. Not only had you not poisoned him against me, Doctor; it was obvious that he did not even know that I had lost access to my files.

"What luck," Jarvik said. "I was going to give you a call at your office. I've a little piece of work for you. Come in, come in."

I asked him if we could take a walk around the block. I could imagine the Sunday lunch about to be served in there, the inspector's kids making a hullabaloo, his wife in her wheelchair, her relatives hovering nearby, all of them preparing to sit down at the table and devour each other. I promised him that my problem would not take up much time.

"I almost called you today," Jarvik said, shutting the door and starting off with me. "It's an urgent case. There are too many other people trying to solve it."

"If I can be of assistance." Although I had no intention of helping him. 'Who is it this time?"

"Here's the photo," Jarvik said, taking an envelope from his pocket and passing it to me.

I put the envelope away without looking at it. "I'll have an answer by Thursday," I answered, selecting the day when I was sure to be far from this former inspector and just as far from this country.

"Don't you want to take a look?" those scissored, mathematical, exact lips of his demanded.

I opened the envelope to cut the conversation short.

It was a photo of Oriana. Her photo at four and a half years old.

Just my bad luck. No image taken by someone else could capture her as I would have; but if the snapshot had been at least a recent one, no matter how ungraceful the photographer, I might have had some clue to understanding that adult Oriana, that perverse woman from whom my childlike Oriana had fled. It was of no use to have a pale, indistinct, ineffective photo of the very same warm-blooded girl that my body had been conquering and exploring in my own bed less than two hours ago. And whom I hoped was still there. Because if Jarvik was looking for her, then it was true that she was really in danger; if he, and who knows what other men, were on the trail, it was going to be more complicated than I had presumed to cross the border with her. Not only that: how could I possibly take your photograph, Marvorelli? How to enter your most private chambers with Oriana by my side, now that I could never again leave her alone at home? Two days after having made fun of Patricia's despair, I was reduced to her selfsame defenselessness. Or perhaps even worse: if Jarvik began to apply to me those exceptional observational powers that had made him the most famous detective in the country, if he began to suspect that I was hiding the very woman he was seeking . . . He was already surprised by the time I was taking with the damned photograph.

"So you'll crack the case by Thursday?" Jarvik asked, but his thin lips exhaled sarcasm. As if they were tasting my hesitancy.

I tried to make my voice stay calm. "And this girl. What did she do?"

"I'm looking for the adult, not for the girl."

Since it was no longer possible to get the dossier from him, as had been my original intention, I used the occasion to attempt to squeeze whatever additional information about Oriana he might have. "You haven't got a more recent shot?" I asked.

"That's the only one." A slit of mistrust began to form in the former inspector's eyes. I had never before shown any interest in any of the cases he had brought me. They must have done something, I supposed, those men, those women, if the police were after them. I never asked about them. And now, only because it was so unprecedented that he should have passed me the photograph of a child, was it possible to add yet one more comment without, or so I hoped, awakening his misgivings.

"She doesn't seem very threatening," I said.

"Appearances," Jarvik answered. "If you knew what she . . .

"What she . . ."

"If you trace her, I'll tell you the whole story. As far as I know it. And that's a promise." And with this, Jarvik stopped in front of his apartment building. We had walked around the block. "But maybe you'd like to tell me what's eating you up?"

While we strolled along, I had been debating with myself how to get into your hospital, Doctor, now that I would be burdened by Oriana's presence. It was a situation I had never had to live: the girl I loved and protected was gradually turning me into a visible man. I felt, of a sudden, as if a sign or a scar had started to grow in the absence that I call my face, something that would identify me, something that would stop me from passing through all doors as I always had. To take that photo I was going to need help and that help at this point could come only from Jarvik. There was no one else. Risky? Not if you know people's secret faces, not if you have discovered the threads with which to pull them.

And I had Jarvik trapped. Jarvik was going to swallow the absurd story I would concoct for him because he was, in the final analysis, a sentimental bastard. I had surmised it since our first encounter in the coffee shop, and I had confirmed it later when I took the precise snapshot of his face pulverized by weakness. Discreet, that snapshot. From a distance, that snapshot. I didn't want him realizing what I was doing. Because I had caught him in a tedious coupling with his invalid wife—and it was so clear that he did not love her

and so clear that she bored him and so clear that he remained with
her out of pity. Afterward, I studied those features from close up,
carefully inspecting that face which was melting in the fatigue of
a sexual act that afforded him no pleasure, that face which became
flabby just before his genitals became tame and flaccid themselves.
Mashed potatoes, I thought, with satisfaction. In spite of the sever-
ity that his visage announced, in spite of the propaganda that his
steel-like lips trumpeted, he was a softy, a tender heart, a man
who cries with the soaps and jumps into fights on the side of the
underdogs. In other words, on the side of the losers. Under so much
supposed firmness, mushy emotionalism. Unable to hurt someone
who is downcast. In order to fool him, to get him to suspend that
mind of his which analyzed and penetrated everything, it would
be enough to feed him some romantic nonsense.

"Inspector, I'm . . . well, you've noticed, no doubt, that I don't
speak much about myself. But the truth, Inspector, is that there
is a woman who . . . well, I like her. I would rather, for obvious
reasons, not reveal her name. I am trying to convince her that she
should not undergo an operation with . . . do you know a surgeon
called Miravelli?"

"Mavirelli?" The former inspector corrected me, letting a skim
of curiosity run down his face like paint. "Has she got some sort
of sickness in her face?"

"She thinks she's . . . ugly, Inspector."

In order to build a solid lie, Doctor—you know this better
than I do, you who make a new deception out of each old face you
operate—one must always start out with a nucleus of truth. So I
allowed myself to evoke Alicia while I talked to Jarvik—Alicia and
not Oriana. I knew that the passion, and the pain, that would seep
into my eyes would shake him. "She's a fool. She compares herself
to the TV stars who sell panty hose and convertibles and tropical
vacations. She wants a new face."

"Tell her," Jarvik erupted, "that to be beautiful all you need is
the love of one person."

Those were the words I was expecting from him. Those were the
words I had once dared timidly to murmur to Alicia.

I went on. "I've gone to visit her every day this week," my deceiving throat said to Jarvik, "and she won't listen to me. But this

morning, I went to see her this morning, and the poor thing had her face all bandaged up. Already. The operation's going to be on Tuesday and she's already . . . I couldn't stand it."

"Go and talk to her again," insisted Jarvik, moved as if he were speaking to somebody he had once loved. "Tell her that beauty comes from inside. Tell her that doctors do not have magical solutions."

"That's what I told her." And it was true. That was what I had told Alicia. "And I must have been convincing, because she gave me one last chance." Although Alicia had not given me that last chance. "And that is why, sir, I need your help."

"It has never been said of me," Jarvik separated each word as if it were a watermelon seed that had to be spat out, "that I was not ready to help someone in love."

He was about to fall into my trap. So I sweetened the story up some more: "The problem is that she demands proof of my love."

"Like a fairy tale!"

"Like a fairy tale, Inspector. She will consider canceling the operation. If I . . ."

"If you . . ."

"If I can take a snapshot of the doctor in the midst of one of his disgusting operations. It would have to be tomorrow. I have no problem, as you can well imagine, entering the hospital by myself. What is more difficult is getting her inside. And I insist on her accompanying me. Only up to the operating room. She can wait outside. I can take care of the rest. That's what I need you for."

I could read the mistrust written in Jarvik's steady, immutable eyes. His reasoning had not been totally eclipsed: it still flashed warnings to him. And I knew that a man as methodical as he would not believe my sincerity—I who had up to that moment always been so silent, arrogant, reserved—if I did not entice him into the whirlpool of my new persona as victim, as surprising to him as it was to me. To allay his suspicions, he had to see me as essentially debased, as debased as his own wife.

It was not as easy as I had planned it years before, when I had taken that photo, when I whispered to myself that this would be the way to entangle him if some day in the future it became necessary.

Because I have never talked to anyone about my face. I don't like to ask for pity, Doctor. To ask for pity is not that different from trying on the latest fashions to keep your lover, or going to a plastic surgeon to make new friends, not that different from what Jarvik's wife does to him. Now I would have to do it.

Or was there any other way of somebody like me touching the soul of a man like him?

"This . . . it's not exactly easy, Inspector. It will not have escaped you that I'm not what you could call, let us say, handsome, right? To get a woman, any woman, to fix her eyes upon me . . ." All of a sudden I stopped. It became impossible to banish Alicia's face, to elude the words I should have entrusted to someone when Alicia went through that door leading to your consulting room, Mavirelli. Or if I could have talked to her about my face, if I could have begged her to stay with me because of my face. "Inspector! The woman I love has got to witness what I am willing to do for her. It's not enough for me to give her the photo and then receive her thanks. She has to see me. See me. So I will be fixed forever in her memory. Or do you think that with this face . . ."

In my lifeless eyes he must have read an abandonment that was not entirely feigned.

His eyes softened.

He felt for me exactly the sort of compassion that I wanted him to feel.

Of course to invite someone into your intimacy, Doctor, has the disadvantage that the someone may end up accepting that invitation. That is what happened with former Inspector Jarvik. Because if I had managed to get him to heed my preposterous story, it was also true that he felt authorized to meddle in my personal affairs. It is the price you pay for demanding a favor.

"I would like to suggest something to you. I hope you don't mind."

There was in his voice—how to describe it so I won't appear, myself, as a sentimental bastard, so you won't get the wrong idea about me, Doctor—there was something almost affectionate, almost sweet. It was the first friendly advice anyone had ever offered me in my entire life. I did not answer him, but something that was not neutral in my eyes must have stimulated him, because he continued: "If you really want to win over a little woman, there is one sort of strategy that never fails. Do you know what it might be?" And when he realized that I was not disposed to answer, that I had no notion of what he was talking about: "A smile," Jarvik said. "Just that. Everybody remembers somebody who smiles. And I have noticed, if you don't mind my observation, that you never smile. Or am I wrong?"

Perhaps in another life, on another planet, inside another universe, I could have been the friend of a man like that. Now it was not possible. Nor would it be possible tomorrow. If he was softly opening up the doors of an affection that I did not need, it was his problem, not mine. What I needed from him I had already gotten: a promise of his help. I kicked shut, I closed, I locked those sterile doors. "I am not diseased, Inspector," I said to him, and if he felt it like a slap in the face, I felt it to be a farewell at the very moment when I said it. "I will smile when I have reason to smile."

So I treated him as I have treated everybody else who has crossed my vision. Like a sleeping woman that you can do anything to. Because he was blind and I was awake. He pitied me and I despised him. Because it was my fate to survive and his fate to serve me.

So he was that observant? He never conjectured that the woman he was looking for so importunately was none other than the friend with the bandaged face who accompanied me the next day to the hospital, who passed with us all the barriers you have set up to keep out the curious, Doctor. So analytic, was he? He didn't realize that, not content with poking my camera into your private operating room, I used the occasion to quickly copy the supposedly nonexistent list of your more important patients, Doctor. So implacable, the former inspector? I made him play the cuckold's role of my beloved's guardian, taking care of her while I was inside, aware that, chained to his honor, he would not direct one word to the nameless woman he had by his side.

Just so you don't get the wrong impression, Doctor: I did not trust him. Not him, not anybody, Doctor. Jarvik could not have coaxed even a phrase out of Oriana. Nor could your nurse out there, at this very moment as we talk to each other in here, make her open her mouth. I have trained her well. Whoever asks you about your bandages, I told her repeatedly, you answer that if it had been your wish to reveal details about your identity, you would not wear them. Or do you want those men to find you?

So don't think that tomorrow I could not once more penetrate your security system, Doctor, that I could not take a new photo that would penetrate the security system you call a face, Doctor. All alone. Without help from Jarvik. Without help from anybody. Though for now, and you will have to agree with me, this should be sufficient.

You'll notice, Miervadelli, that not one of your assistants prevented me from taking this snapshot. I wonder why you bother to hire them? So many of them and all so useless. Perhaps good apprentices of medical care, but as watchdogs—get rid of them. Not one of them perceived that there was a stranger among them in the operating room. They may have been too busy with the patient, Colonel Zagasto's wife—I had no problem recognizing her. She always appeared on television. The viewers seemed not to understand that the clinic she was opening, or the school, or the park, or the avenue, were the same ones that had been on last week and that only the name had been changed. Her advisers probably didn't want to waste their time changing her speech, which was the same idiocy she had read a couple of days back. Fortunately, she did not open her mouth while I was in there. She might have bored me to death. I was lucky: she was asleep when I arrived and was still asleep a few minutes later, when you came in.

Your operating mask worried me. But I was sure, let me tell you, or maybe it was a mere intuition, that at some finale of your intervention, you would tear that piece of cloth off and reveal that one face of yours which had been indelibly marked by an inner demon, that face upon which, as on a blackboard, even a small kid could read what your burning and sunken eyes were really thinking. The camera should not spring into action until that moment arrived. And that's how it went. I crouched with utter calm in my corner, waiting for the curtains to rise on your face, Doctor, with my machine hidden, just in case, underneath the white smock that Jarvik had handed me. Some ten minutes later, when the patient had been entirely split open, with that silence which bones exude when they are at their most naked, glimmering under that arc of lights, you made a slight gesture with your left hand, and, as if miraculously, your assistants disappeared. Even the anesthetist fled. They were so quick and efficient about it that I had no doubt this was not the first time they had been asked to leave the room during an operation. What you did to Colonel Zagasto's wife, have you done it—or am I way off target?—to your other patients? Did you do it to Alicia? And do your assistants leave you alone because you have convinced them that you possess some sort of magical procedure that nobody else can witness, something that guarantees the happy outcome of the operation? We were left alone, Doctor, I in the shadows and you under the reflectors and the woman sprawled on the table between us, like rotten earth which a pair of dark birds was going to dispute. When you lowered your mask, Doctor, as if you were taking off your trousers, my camera knew that not much time was left and also that, once again, my eyes had not erred. You began to advance, with the graveyard of your face open on the openness of that woman's face, advancing toward her with eyes that boiled with the insects of an unnamable desire, and I thought for an instant that you were going to make love to her and that this was the secret I would capture forever. But the photograph I have is more interesting, Maraville. It is a pleasure to confirm that your aberrations are much more intense and profound than those of the mere flesh, and that you will be more than willing to negotiate an agreement with me, which will give you more power and will give more of Oriana to me.

It is possible, therefore, that you know, as I do, master surgeon, that one's real sex does not reside between the legs but further up, in those eyes that were watching the face of that skinless woman exposed like a soiled heart in the middle of the road. Your hands descended, Doctor, toward the entrails of that face, and when they were about to penetrate them, when the violation was about to be consummated, my camera seized the exact instant before it—and what can be seen between your fingers is a tiny metallic apparatus, which you were on the verge of placing inside some space in Mrs. Zagasto's skull. It is not quite clear where, Doctor, in the snapshot, see for yourself. Only don't touch the celluloid, please. I must presume it is in the cavern that yawns behind the nose, that communicates upward to the brain and the eyelids, that controls the tongue and what is said and what is listened to, some recess

that must be the geographic center of the personality. My eyes first
and then my hands and the pale film in my brain after that and
the orgasm of the shuddering trigger of the camera at last and I
had you, Doctor— your face like a gigantic mouth turned inside
out like a glove of skin, and the woman like a wedding cake that
someone has crushed and that will nevertheless soon be eaten to
the last dreg, and above all the undeniable shining of that thing
which you situated in the most private part of that patient in order
to—what do you do with that insignificant mechanism, Doctor?
Do you spy on people? Do you give them orders? Or do you merely
listen to their most intimate conversations?

When I finish talking to you, in a few more minutes, Doctor,
I'd really like to know.

But I see no need to point out that it is not in your interest for
anyone else to get this photo. In exchange for not sending it, to the
colonel or to any of your other clients, the services I require from
you are exceptionally paltry. A modest monthly sum deposited in
a foreign bank and, right now, an insignificant amount, which will
help us take care of urgent matters: my plans are to travel tomorrow evening. And because I understand that business deals work
only if both parties are gaining, each week you will receive, Doctor,
from abroad, one photograph from my collection. You may well
ask, of what use will they be? I'm astonished, Mirevedelski. What
I'm giving you is an authentic gallery of human privacy—thousands of faces at their worst, their most intolerable. You can use the
photos for blackmail, if you wish; but I suggest that they can serve
you better by helping you further disguise that vileness—they will
be like the counterpart of each lovely feature that you have been
modeling with your chirurgical hygiene. Study those leers, that
nudge, this wink, the mad pantomime with which people betray
their concealed emotions. Study them to learn how to erase them
from the humanity that comes before you. You must stretch that
skin, stretch the falseness, the terseness of that skin, stretch it so
tightly that not one of the subterranean gestures that are vegetat-
ing below can escape.

As for my departure from this country, I wouldn't mind having
a medical certificate signed by you, Doctor. Just write that anybody
who takes the bandages off this patient runs a high risk of infec-

tion. That should be enough, and your fame and influence, Doctor, to guarantee that we'll be able to pass under the very noses of the men who are trying to reach my girl before Jarvik does.

And, of course, Oriana will, in effect, be needing those bandages.

You see this photograph? This one? The one that the former inspector gave me, Oriana as a child?

What I want, Doctor, is for you to return this face and this age to Oriana's body. While I assist you. No one else can be present. I want her exactly, and forever, as she appears in this photograph. There are other faces at work inside her, Mavirelli, swimming beneath her innocence, trying to come up for air.

I want you to suffocate them, Doctor.

Well, Doctor? Oriana is waiting for us outside. Shall we go and undress her?

What do you say?

SECOND

As for me, I am still enclosed in this kingdom that I built for myself.

When you think of it, it wasn't due to my memory. It was due to my hands. Because adults also told me, as they have told every child in the world, that we arrive here with hands that belong to us. The difference is that I always knew it was not true.

I knew it at birth. The first thing I saw were those two men waiting at the foot of the bed. The same ones that had come to visit me, some time before I was born.

You don't remember them? A pair of men always in a hurry, blunt, and always in a hurry? The real owners of my hands, of all the hands in the universe? With their deeds to the property? With their knives? With their photos? I had no hands when they came to see me. If you want them to be born whole and healthy, they said, you'd better rent a couple. You can pay on the installment plan, they said. On the condition that you return them the day you die. And that's when they showed me the photographs of the people who had rejected their offer. Beggars' stumps. Fingerless babies. Hemiplegics. Paralyzed limbs. So that those images would not anguish me for the rest of my life, they promised I would forget that conversation. According to them I would live, like everyone else, with the illusion that my hands belonged to me.

In that, however, they were wrong. Because I remembered them at my birth. My father did not see the men, my mother did not see them. Only I realized when they began to approach. I shut my eyes so they would not know that I had recognized them from before.

"Seems like she's got them in good shape," the bigger one said.

"Hurry up," said the other one. "We've got a lot more to inspect. They reproduce like rabbits, this rabble . . ."

"Lucky they also die," the bigger one answered and looked straight at my papa.

"Yeah. Not much time left."

Almost five years later, when papa died, I saw them again.

I had spent my infancy trying to convince myself that these men did not exist. But at nighttime, I dreamt of them. They were just as I had glimpsed them that first time in my mama's cavern. Except that in my dreams they had grown more hands and I had grown old. I was lying in an open field. It was midnight. Suddenly, as if they were lights in a theater, someone turned off the stars. And that enormous double silhouette darkened the horizon, and then those multiple arms crawled toward what had been my body and I could feel their ice descending down my shoulders and my arms, and if I was lucky, papa would awaken me.

"What did you dream, little one?"

So much love, so much weariness in his voice. I did not have to listen to those men to know that he was going to die.

"I don't remember."

"If you tell me, you'll feel better."

They could not be far away. Perhaps in the next room. And if I revealed their existence, they would come to take my very own hands, even before I had passed away. So he was the one who had to comfort me with some incident from his life, a fairy tale where somebody saves the girl when everything seems lost. Even today I can repeat, word for word, each story he told me. I have kept them here alive in my kingdom.

That would happen—if I was lucky.

Because the sicker papa became and the more harried my mama, the less they worried about waking me from my nightmares. And then I had to witness and watch in my dreams what those men would do to my hands, what they would do to my hands the day I died.

They tied the dead doves of my hands to a rope as if they were afraid of catching a contagious disease. Complaining bitterly that I had ruined them. When they had been consigned to me, they were new and decent and now they were haggard and played out.

"My poor treasures," the bigger one muttered as if they were a pair of strangled dogs. "Look what they've done to you."

They washed my hands. I had to witness how their many arms soaped the fingernails and the fingers that had been mine, what used to be my knuckles and the palms. I watched them fracturing the music of that skin. Stuffing my pretty hands into a huge pot of boiling water, extracting them as pale as sheets. Without a wrinkle. Without a line that could remind anyone of what they had once caressed.

Really dead now.

And they would cast them, like throatless birds, into a heap with thousands of other hands. It was only then that I realized that, behind me, by my side, near and in the shadows, other eyes were accompanying me. My parents, my cousins, the men and women I would get to know if my life were long enough, those people my hands would travel with if I could keep them.

We were never able to discover their final destination. We did not dare, even in a dream, to follow those men when they lowered themselves into a vast cellar where people graced with only two hands were bound to lose their way. We remained behind with our voices to keep us company. Our hands, white as death, blurred and without history, were now going to start a journey toward the arms of the children who were about to be born. So that no child could know what had come before, what her ancestors had danced. So that we would forget.

I would awaken by myself, with my hands intact and loving, with those voices still whispering in my ears, truer than the pillow, than the early song of birds at dawn, than the sad footsteps of my mother going to give papa his medicine. That's what they use the hands for, the voices said to me: to punish whoever betrays the terms of the contract. It's what will happen to you if you ever tell this secret.

I would get up and go to my papa's bed.

I was too small to gather him into my arms. The only thing I could receive from him was his melody, the rhythm of his memories. I had already noticed that people treat their memory as if it were an endless garbage deposit. They stuff themselves with the past and then defecate it.

I was different.

When those men arrived to get my papa's hands, I had already labored at length to keep the memories clean and intact.

I had spent my infancy trying to convince myself that the men did not exist. But I was not surprised when they came in the door a few moments before papa stopped breathing. Mama cried quietly, her face hidden, her shoulders downcast. I did not turn to look at them.

"Just on time," the smaller one said. "Hurry up."

The other took off his hat with respect. "With your permission, sir," he said to my papa's sealed eyes, "but we have a contractual obligation to carry out." And then, rapidly, he withdrew the hands as if they were a couple of gloves. Nobody, not even mama, could have perceived that those hands had been ravaged. Their shell was still there—enough to fool any inspection.

And then, unexplainably, papa's face, as begrimed and old and cracked as his hands, opened into a smile.

"What's with this one?" the smaller one asked. "How come the happiness?"

"What do you care? If he wants to die cheerful, what's it to us?"

The smaller one hesitated for another instant. He walked his eyes around my parents' bedroom. I felt for a moment that gaze slapping my skin and passing like the hot air of a fan. Then he left.

I heard them moving down the stairs. I heard them on the way to that place I had seen only in dreams.

It was then that papa died. With the smile still on his lips. Because he had had the last word. The hands of my papa would not be useful to those men: not to infiltrate the lives of the unborn children, not as the hands of a soldier to hurt rebels, not for anything. Let them take his hands to their washroom and cellar. They would be unable to erase even so much as a scar. Someone had listened to the secret cantata of those hands, giving refuge to each line, rocking each memory in a cradle, singing the couplets that this man's mouth would never more pronounce.

That someone was me.

I was young, less than five, but the first time he confided in me, an intimate secret, talking to me as you talk to children when you think they cannot understand, as so many have talked to me during these years, that first time I knew that if the resonance of his voice floated on the surface of my mind, for everybody to see, when those men came to get the hands, they were going to carry away my memories along with his.

At the moment of my papa's death, I should have rushed to bury his story in some depth of myself, should have covered it with all the earth in the universe. So inside my fear that nobody would ever find it. But something inside me had muttered no, that if I had thrown his hands into the grave, I would never be able to retrieve them. So young I was and I already knew that memories can rot as quickly as a body. Quicker.

At that very moment those men were testing my papa's hands, and the boiling pot was proving unable to whiten them; at that moment they were asking themselves about that final mysterious smile, and, without another word between them, they were starting out on the way back to my home.

I ran to my own room and waited by the high window that looks out on the street. And yes, a while later they appeared. They were coming up the avenue, arguing, cursing one another, each blaming the other for what had happened. When they stopped in front of the door to our house, they let their hands speak. That was when they took out those knives. As if out of the air. As if they were leaping from inside the fingers.

They entered without knocking.

I could hear them down there, opening and closing drawers, overturning furniture, ripping up cushions, slashing portraits. Room by room, down there. Coming nearer.

They began to mount the stairs.

They were looking for a tape, some notes, papers. Something concrete, something that made a sound, something written. The ephemeral resources with which adults preserve a past that escapes them. Those two men were looking for something they could read and burn, touch and burn, hear and burn.

In the room next door they tied mama to a chair. She would not remember later, but they tied her to a chair, asking her where that smile had come from. Only when they had searched the house from top to bottom did they drag their legs in my direction.

I had nothing to offer them.

After they had kicked open the door to my room, the only thing that those two men saw was a girl of almost five backed against a wall. A girl who did not even have permission to cross the street. A girl playing with a panda that her grandfather had given her. She did not lift her eyes. It was as if she could not see them.

I was not the one who was in that room. It was Oriana.

A moment before the door opened, a moment before having to expose my father's hands to the eyes of those two men and to their knives, I had retreated to the last wall of my room. I felt behind me the hard barrier of cement through which my body could not pass. There was no longer anywhere to flee.

There was no longer anywhere. But when the door opened, I took a step backward.

And watched them, from here. I watched them tear the panda's plush. I watched them undress the little girl's body with their eyes. I watched them place the angle of a flashlight in the most hidden of that body's seven holes.

I did not care. I was already in this kingdom where I now find myself, this kingdom I have inhabited ever since. It was not a kingdom back then. It was not even a house.

Over the years I built the rest. Anyone could have done it. But people fall in love with the cities where their feet can take strides, where their lungs can breathe, the cities full of beings as driven as they are. From here I watch them. I too journeyed afterward to those cities which they call real. I also journeyed there to collect their lives, to read what their hands had sung, to sink myself into their eyes that were about to be snuffed out. I like the dead, the people who are about to die. They ask for nothing more than to be relieved of their voices. They ask for nothing more than to die with a smile.

I did not know that I would have to build a whole kingdom. When I started, I knew only that I needed a secure place to gather my papa's words. I took my time transplanting them to the bedroom I was building inside myself. When that space was filled with my father's phrases and still his stories kept on spilling over as if from a fountain, I went on with the rest of the house. And in each room I would put one of his melodies, and when there were no more rooms left, I simply continued, adding imaginary halls and invented towers and endless furnishings. Some children build their father a tomb. I built him a palace to lodge the sounding shadows of his hands as he tendered them to me. It was enough to know that to be with him again I need only enter that palace and stroll through it with the slowness of the slowest of pianos. The proof was in the smile. Papa had died with the certainty that his hands, at the end, belonged only to him.

But the real house where I had passed the first five years of my existence was in ruins. I watched those men opening the legs of that girl where I had taken up residence since my birth. And I could not do it. I could not return to that body.

At that moment I promised that years later I would return to that little thing leaning against an unyielding wall. But at that moment I knew it to be too dangerous. Let those two waste their years spying on Oriana. I was going to prepare my kingdom, I was going to distribute my papa's calm and defiant smile as if it were the wind. Out there, beyond Oriana's sad voice that was singing alone to itself, beyond the ballad that she rippled to herself in order to sleep, I could hear, in the miserable cities where people are not the owners of their own hands, thousands of men, thousands of women, who awaited me.

It took me more than a decade to ready the sanctuaries where I could preserve the residue of their lives. I did not approach them until my kingdom was in place.

At the beginning they were, they had to be, people those men could never associate with me. Later it would be possible, I thought, to receive other voices, closer, more intimate voices. But I began with the tramps, the unemployed, the fugitives, the solitary and unmarried domestics, the blind who passed their days in the plaza listening to the wings of crows, the sick agonizing in the dampest recesses of the worst hospitals. I made Oriana, when she was old enough to go out by herself, walk through those neighborhoods. And I located my loved ones by that sorrow that human beings sweat when the body glimpses, though not yet the mind, that they are going to die. The hour of their death was written on their hands. I visited them awhile before that hour came. I demanded of Oriana no more than an attentive ear and a compassionate face.

As for me, I supplied my memory and my kingdom. And when the sounds of those hands had been registered, we left, as soon as we could, through the back door, before those two men came in through the front. Of my presence, of Oriana's footsteps, they never found a trace. What they found, invariably, blooming greenly in the desert of the dying face, was a smile.

At times I would stay in the area, asking Oriana to keep a prudent distance—so that I could relish the violent despair of those two men. At such moments, the only thing I missed was someone with whom I could share their defeat. With one more person, with two, with three, I might one day go further still, I might follow those men to their hideaway, descend into that cellar where the hands of all the human beings who had lived in this world lay, with four, with five minds such as my own, I might initiate the rescue of those other voices, so that the living could discover what the dead had once upon a time murmured. But in the puddle at Oriana's feet only her solitary face was reflected. Nobody, nothing more.

It was Oriana who wanted me to keep living in my kingdom. She obeyed me when I whispered to her to get up, to smooth her dress, to go and untie mama. Just as, years later, when I needed her muscles in order to go out and gather the voice of an old woman who was peeling potatoes in the devastation of a kitchen and who was about to die as helpless and exposed as one of the potatoes she was peeling, Oriana also agreed. But she did not invite me to lodge in her body forever. I was no more than a passenger. Yes. She was the one. She was the one who did not want us to become one person again, she the one who decided to stagnate endlessly on the threshold of five. She was the one who, as her body grew, refused to mature, refused to bear children, refused to be an adult.

I did not contradict her. It was for her own good. Her childhood innocence saved her from becoming the sluice through which so much pain came, the pain of others that I flushed into me. And it made people trust her, sure that someone of that countenance, transparent as a child, would not betray them. I did not complain. I'll admit it. I preferred it like that.

I lacked the wisdom to understand that between us a frontier of ice and resentment was gradually extending itself. But there was no other body I could employ. There was no other way of salvaging those voices. And did she have another use, a better use, for her life? What more did she want than to be the elder sister to those neglected words, to be the savior, the confessor, almost a saint? What more can anybody want?

Only now do I know that somebody can want considerably more than that, can want to be more than the tunnel for another person's light, more than the repository for someone else's memories.

I should have realized that she had a mind of her own, but I did not even understand how frightened she was. I could have sensed it that morning decades after our father's death, when mama woke us up, woke her up and woke me up, the mother we had shared the way we shared a body. As soon as I felt her hands in Oriana's hair I knew, with the clarity with which one remembers the past rather than the vague penumbra with which you predict the future, I knew that mama had only three years left to live. I knew it before Oriana opened her eyes. It was something in the absent trembling of the hands, as if they were trying to caress me underwater, already distant. If not then, at least that evening, when for the first time Oriana imprisoned me in my kingdom, I should have realized how her fear would lead her to rebel.

There had been, however, no lack of signs. Though she had never sabotaged even one of my encounters with the thousands of anonymous beings who were dying in their remote beds, the few times I had timidly proposed to rescue the serenata that might be concealed in the hands of people who were more familiar, nearer to us, her reaction had been categorical. She would walk away.

That morning some sort of anguish in my voice must have alerted her. When I murmured to those motherly hands in our hair that I would harvest them before they were eradicated, when I told them not to be sad. How was I to allow those men to boil to the bones those soft guardians that had washed us, nourished us? Of course Oriana had understood the consequences of my plans before I could formulate the plans themselves: again the multiplication of crawling hands in the night, again the steps of those men approaching the room where she was leaning against an unrelenting wall.

But mama's hands! The hands of the only one who had never lost hope that Oriana might get better. The hands of the first who realized, a bit after her father's death, that the girl was not reacting well. Those hands which had tried, unsuccessfully, to teach Oriana how to read, to add two plus two, to pull her out of that perpetual infancy into which she had fallen. Those hands that had been driven to the task of persuading teachers, uncles, psychologists, specialists, doctors, that there was a solution, the hands that had formed a human net that would protect the child if something happened to her mother, the hands that had never given up.

I observed her efforts from afar. Absorbed in my own projects, I knew that someday it would be my turn to gather from her own lips her struggle for Oriana, to settle her hands by the side of so many other memories, which filled the infinite coffers of my kingdom.

It was toward that burial ground next to papa's that I departed on the morning when I understood, when we both understood, that mama was dying. Without knowing that the same evening I would be unable to find the road back to Oriana's body. I opened the door that led to the outer world and the room into which I stepped was the same one I had just left. I crossed it, opened the door again, and the same endless blind alley of rooms repeated itself on the other side. Fear did not have time to shake me. At the third attempt, Oriana gave me access to her lovely domains. During what might have been less than a minute, I had found myself absolutely cut off from Oriana's eyes, from her throat, from her legs, from what her fingers were combing. Alone, just as I am now alone—but now it is forever.

I did not understand, I did not want to understand, the danger. I had always kept a window that looked out upon her existence, a floating fragment of my mind that allowed me to control what that body in which I dwelled was doing. I interpreted her transitory blockade as an accident, a short circuit that would never be repeated. Precisely because Oriana had no life to reassume, because without me she was nobody, because not a line had been drawn on the palm of her hands, it never occurred to me that this might be her first rehearsal for independence.

So some days later I sat Oriana down, she with the typical demeanor of a small child, at her mother's feet, and then I made her lips flourish into the puerile demand for a story, that Mama should retell the one about the most ancient of our grandparents, and I disposed her body to receive and transfer each syllable from that woman who had given us birth. That was when, without the slightest warning of what Oriana intended to do, I found myself enclosed once again in this kingdom with no gates. I don't know how long it lasted this time. A long time. The time it took mama to complete her story. Because only at that moment, only when mama's thousand and one words had concluded, did Oriana let me go back to her body. She let the slit of an indolent window swing slightly open. Through her distant eyes I could see mama getting up from the sofa, her vocabulary lost forever in the air of the approaching night.

I did not cross toward Oriana.

I remained here in the room where mama's fullness should have been reposing. This empty room inside me, like a womb that cannot bear anything alive.

Thinking, for the first time, of my own extinction.

I had experienced how irremediable the world could be without Oriana. That is how I would remain, vulnerable, bridgeless, shoreless, if something happened to her. And if what happened to her happened to be death, the day in which those men came to get the hands Oriana and I had rented before our birth, that day they would follow her traces underground and into our earth, that day they would also obtain the maps of my kingdom. One by one, threshold by threshold, without my being able to do anything to protect them, house by house, they would exterminate my memories, until my hands would be ready to be hung from some child about to be born, some remote perishing child who would not know of my existence.

If Oriana would not allow me to rescue my mama's hands, would not allow me to come near mama's hands, then, was it not then too late to find someone with whom to deposit all the stories I had gathered, all the stories I remembered so they would not be lost, so I could be the one to pierce forth into a smile when those men approached? I had glimpsed women in the mirror of my dreams, faces that multiplied themselves and reminded me of my own. How could I reach them, exiled from Oriana? How could I join that chain of women I longed for, a chain of women who were not deaf, who had not been born defeated, who had agreed to take charge of the howls of other human beings when they are leaving, leaving?

Did they not exist out there, in some kingdom less invisible than
the one I had dreamt?

It was too late.

There is not much more to tell.

Mama began to get worse. She was unable to care for the creature who looked like a mature woman but was only five years old.
They began to leave Oriana in strange houses, one hand to another,
as if she were a package. A cousin would deposit her at a friend's
and perhaps return for her, perhaps not, and from there she would
be taken to a psychologist and then to an asylum and to another
person or maybe to the same one, or who knows who would come
to fetch her. Masks in the fog. More difficult each time to know
in whose hands we were being placed.

Oriana must have been enchanting and the people must have
had quite a bit of fun with her. For a week. Or two. But people tire
quickly of the innocent, as they do of the ailing and the crestfallen,
and then, you can be sure that to another refuge and another home
and another period of playing she went, as if Oriana herself was
one of the many lives that we had both given shelter to in other
times, so it went, just so.

From time to time we would see Mama again, the anchor that
Mama still was, and I would try to leap toward her, to relieve her,
to prepare her hands for the day when—but the walls of Oriana
are white and cold, as my hands will be in the future after they
have been boiled. I do not know how to climb them. The occasions
when she would allow me out to breathe, to gather the next to the
last music in a dry throat, were becoming less and less frequent,
until one day they ceased entirely.

And I could not guess the identities of those who harbored her,
as if she were a daughter who never writes home. But here in this
growing darkness I wondered if she had not learned on her own
how to give refuge to strange voices, if that was not the way in
which she was paying for her safekeeping.

Because the last time she allowed me to share her gaze, the last
time I awoke outside my kingdom in an alien place, a terribly transitory and real place, there was in front of us a high window and a
street. Through her eyes I saw the plague of those two men advancing. But they were not coming for me or for her. I knew it because

of the absence of an approaching death in the reflection that Oriana returned to me from the glass of the window. They were coming for the hands of someone whom Oriana had comforted, the hands of someone, a man or a woman, who had taken care of her.

And now that person could no longer help her and Oriana did not know how to save herself. So she had called on me. I forced her to look at those men rolling toward us like a sickening tide.

"Run," I told her legs, but they would not immediately obey me. The two of us watched, with eyes that were almost crippled, the avalanche of those men. "Run," I repeated, with the fierceness one must summon to shout at morons who would let themselves burn to death in the middle of a house in flames. "And tell everybody that they are looking for you. Don't forget."

I have not heard from her since. I must suppose that she fled. I must suppose that she listened to me. I suppose it is because those men have not invaded Oriana's body, have not found me. Yet.

It is my only hope. That she will not forget. In the few moments of liberty that she left me, I would demand that she repeat this to her fleeting guardians. Though they might think her mad. But they would not. Her terror could not evoke doubts or frivolous replies. They were going to believe her. It is possible, then, that someone else knows we are in danger.

But would that be a person in whom I could put my trust?

I go to the outskirts of my kingdom and I call from there. Like a wolf that wants to make the sky give birth to the dead moon with its screams. But who will hear me? And if they hear me, who will answer? Who will gather my words as I gathered those who were dying without a moon for their hands in the night?

Even if no one answers, I do not repent.

I did what I had to do. As soon as I was born I knew things that others take a lifetime to learn, that some never know at all. In front of my eyes a trainload of passengers was derailing. In front of my eyes the passengers were bleeding to death. And if I had to soil my immaculately washed sheets, if I had once again to clean that blood with the sheets of my recent birth, I would do it all over again. It is nothing to be proud of. That's the way my life turned out. When a bird falls from a tree, you must return it to its nest. Some do not see the bird, they do not see the tree.

I do not blame them. If they do not answer. If they do not come.

In this kingdom there are no faces, not even my own. Here even the birds that fall from their nests exist only in the memories that were lived by others. People do not walk, traffic signals are not put up, parks are unnecessary. There are only houses and musings and pathways which lead from house to house, and in each house a family of memories sleeps, waiting for me to come visit them. And soon the lights will start to go out, one after the other, like a city that has spent its energy. Going out as the sky went out that night in my dream. And then Oriana's door will open. It will open, not so that I may leave but so that those men may finally enter my last home.

I want you to know it, ladies of my dreams. Though you cannot hear me, though you do not dare open your kingdoms to my voice. I want you to know that the one who is dying now is me. I want you to ask yourselves if I do not have the right to a miracle. If I cannot be rescued, just once, just once, just one single time, the way it came to pass in the fairy tales my father told me.

I want you to ask yourselves.

While in some corner of this city where I cannot walk, my mother and all the mothers of the universe are dying without anybody to listen to their song.

THIRD

I am sure you will forgive me, my friend, if I answer you with a slight tinge of familiarity in my voice. I do have my reasons: it could almost be stated that we are already partners. You do not like the idea? Please. I did not interrupt you until you had finished. And you were not brief.

So, with all due respect, let me inform you that it is my considered opinion that you underestimate us both. You do not demand all that I can give; and you proffer far less than you yourself can deliver. What else am I to deduce? Being the privileged proprietor of that special face, what do you submit as your part of the deal? A miserable batch of photographs. When I have within my reach all those live bodies, you offer these miserable photographs. And knowing the power I have to grant your most extravagant and outrageous desires, what do you ask of me? To travel abroad. Not a good way of doing business, my dear fellow. Not when both sides end up losing.

You decidedly need someone to look after your interests.

I do not blame you for your misgivings. Like you, during all these years I could not conceive that a partner might be an equal. A partner would inevitably sell you to the highest bidder, as your Pareja did when the opportunity arose. Even at the period I would like to talk to you about, even then, when I was a young doctor, just out of medical school, squandering my time as an intern in that mediocre hospital for insignificant people, the certainty I had already formed of my own worth would not allow me to entertain even the notion of an associate. A brilliant career beckoned to me from the future. Someone with your avid eyes would have understood it right away: I was going to be the most eminent plastic surgeon of all time. Yes. Of all time. You do not have the slightest drop of ambition in your veins. You cannot understand anybody's longing to shine. What I yearned for was to defeat even rivals who would appear after my death.

On that afternoon, therefore, when a child was brought to me, a baby who had just been born, it mattered that I knew who I would someday be. The baby seemed ordinary, one might almost venture that it was immeasurably ordinary and yet the nurse who shoved it onto my weighing scales assured me that there was something strange about it, perhaps in its face. She was, she informed me, an extremely responsible employee, but in regard to this little child, she would forget the most elementary tasks. She was not giving him his bottle on time, she wasn't bathing him on schedule, she wasn't taking his temperature.

Oh, no, you don't. Not one interruption. No. Not a word. I let you speak as long as you wanted. It is my turn now.

True, it has been my turn all these years. My turn began at that moment, so many decades ago when that nurse offered up that child into these hands, which you are watching with such intensity. But that's my privilege.

I did not, on that occasion, intend to waste more than five minutes on the case. Why should I attend to that child's problems? Or worry about the nurse's fatigued, overwrought brain? But just in case, I sent her out into the corridor. I might have been inexperienced, but I had already warned myself that it is indispensable to be alone with any patient: our consulting rooms are like temples. Our privacy is what protects us.

So that day, fortunately, there was no one to witness how I examined the boy. His skin, particularly the skin on his face, turned out to be special. What need is there to describe it? You know better than any other human being both its defects and its virtues. I will not lie to you: I was very excited. Never, in the most obscure bibliography or the most meticulous notes, had I ever read of anything quite like this. A chameleon, after all, a butterfly altering its colors, a rabbit shedding its fur according to the seasons, all are creatures programmed for a limited, cyclical register of environments and habitations. But that a human being would be able to fuse with his ever-changing backgrounds, could mix in to the point of invisibility . . .

Even at that moment I was aware that the commercial possibilities were, for all practical purposes, infinite. For leisure, for love, for work, for journalism, for military uses: unlimited. Do not interrupt. I know what you are about to say: of course nobody in their right mind would wish to remain in that condition permanently. I had chosen my specialization precisely because I knew that people kill, lie, betray, accumulate millions, decide whom they will marry and who will be their friends, with the sole objective of achieving prominence, of being seen. Show me a beggar who does not dream of becoming an emperor.

Who would want to admit, as you already have, in fact, that one is dead before having had the chance to live? But on a transitory basis, my good man—that is altogether another story. For a criminal or a policeman, for a spy or someone who fears spies, for a husband who cheats on his wife or who wants to see with his own eyes if she is faithful to him. I had, as yet, not one client; nevertheless, I knew what they would give to be able to saunter unseen among their employees, their subjects, their voters, their pupils, their rivals. I could already picture myself. Having altered their faces into loveliness and instant media recognition, I would invest them with an additional momentary invisibility, so that they could find out whom to trust and against whom to act, so that they could have private vacations where nobody could identify them, so that they could wield more power than they had ever conceived of.

But my own dreams of fortune and fame did not last long. A few seconds, to be exact. The chemical substance (or if you want to call it magical, I don't mind) within that skin would be useless to me if I told the hospital about it. Just as I had automatically chosen to discard that silly nurse, just as it had never crossed my mind to let her share one cent of the profits, that is just how my superiors would exclude me from the deal. I was as new to that profession as that little boy was new to the world. Other surgeons would operate on him, others would get their pictures in the papers and on the evening news. I would get—if I was lucky, that is—a footnote, some trivial reference in a medical encyclopedia. Unless . . .

That is right. Unless I kept the secret of that skin till more propitious days. Unless I simply let the wrapping paper with which that child had come to this earth, unless I let it grow with all the dark liberty it could muster, and I were able to appropriate it much later, when I would have the resources to insure its adequate exploitation. It did not occur to me and you can see that I was not amiss—that someone half visible would have any trouble surviving.

I proceeded to tell the nurse, therefore, that the child could not be in a healthier condition, and that she was the one in need of medical attention, preferably of the psychiatric variety, because she seemed on the verge of a *surmenage*. As for me, I was nobly ready to overlook her repeated failure to care well for the infant. If she talked about the matter with anyone else, however, I would be obliged to bring charges against her. So this consultation was not even noted in your files or in mine. That is why you did not discover it when you began to research your past.

Which does not mean, my friend, that I let you go your merry way without following your trail. Although you were not to produce dividends until twenty years later, you were somewhat of an investment, were you not, a future factory? I can remember that at a certain moment one of my more subtle interventions even became necessary. The first time they took you back to the hospital for a harried checkup, I took care to alter the results of the laboratory tests—making sure that nobody investigated what ailed you. I am not attributing to myself credit that in all fairness belongs mainly to you. But neither do I deny that, with all discretion, whenever it became indispensable, I spent my scant revenue to close the door that might have led you into the public light. And, in effect, here you are, like a tiger ready to be embalmed.

At first I would visit you regularly, with a mixture of gratification and anguish similar to that with which people open the stock-market pages in the paper, sure that no matter how long it might take, a day would come when your hide, like that tiger's, would again be available and, this time, profitable. But later, my visits became less frequent. On my own, without having to skin you for a profit, I was getting on splendidly in my profession. I may have been overly confident. I was inspired by the vision of a world where the people who appear in the news, the prominent people, the people that matter, yes, indeed, that they should all be as shining and bubbly as the unbelievably enticing angels who each day provoke us in the soft-drink ads.

As a child, I had always hated ugly people, with their defective eyes, their tortured nostrils, their repugnant pelt. It was an unfair imposition, especially if they happened to be the sort of person who had acquired some degree of notoriety. Repulsive insects like them, I told myself, should conceal themselves, or at least should make the effort to transfigure their visage. I would be, I swore, the instrument for that transfiguration. I would be the provider of embellishment and grace for the pre-eminent men and women of our time. Quite a responsibility, wouldn't you say?

This crusade for a society in which power would always be exercised with the accountability of beauty did not make me forget you totally, but I will be the first to admit that you began to grow distant, perhaps pale, setting behind the horizon of my priorities. It had always been irksome to follow your wake, but now, as I concentrated on matters that seemed more immediately advantageous, to locate you was becoming more difficult and impractical. In some page of my inner calendar, I knew that your high school graduation was drawing near and that it would be the key date to present myself to you, to propose a covenant. But when you graduated, I was in the middle of the most promising transaction of my whole career. You boast of the fact that you care not a bit about politics, so I will not tire you. Nor would confidentiality allow it. But there are certain things you might as well know—it will affect the way in which you consider the counteroffer that I soon shall put before you. So you can realize that I do have the means to defend you and, if you insist, your transient mate as well.

Some time after I left the hospital, a rather grayish sort of client came to see me. Quite a common person—but with one idea that I do not hesitate to qualify as an act of sheer genius. You are not interested in names or you forget them, so I do not intend to fill your head with insignificant syllables. It is enough to say that the man knew only one thing well in the world: he knew the face that he wanted to have manufactured for himself. He had invested all his money in polls. But not in order to guess people's tastes, their opinions, their political preferences. The only thing that mattered, he said, the only thing he needed in order to be successful, was the

exact face that people at a certain moment in history were expecting. And at that moment he had discovered the popular demand
for a curious blend of juvenile features with a serene and mature
gaze. That is what everybody longed for at the time. I rearranged
his grandfatherly sunken cheeks, I made his eyes so sweet a blue
that they would seem incapable of swatting a fly, I grafted deter-
mination and innocence onto his bland jaw. He specified what he
wanted, but I made the sauce. And his success was spectacular.

It was auspicious that I had already elaborated the revolution-
ary method whereby we can curtail the time it takes to alter a face.
What my ads say—that we can change everything in somebody's
physiognomy in less than half an hour—happens to be absolutely
true. But what started out as a strategy for the industrialization of
gorgeousness ended up by allowing me, in the case of this client,
to compose incessantly, without interfering with losses of time, the
everyday adjustments that he required. An early fifteen minutes
with me and he was remodeled for the day. An austere wrinkle
added over here, a mischievous radiance over there, and the man
he saw in the mirror was exactly the one that the opinion polls
suggested would be popular. What was he? A senator, a president,
a lieutenant colonel, a TV anchorman, the manager of the largest
corporation? That should not concern us here. Thanks to the skill
of his opinion polls and of my hands, we had discovered a way to
keep him in his post forever.

Or at least that is what we believed. But one day my client,
venerable as a statesman, exuberant as an adolescent, came to see
me, rather perturbed. For some time now his secret polls stub-
bornly insisted on the weariness of his multiple admirers or fans.
They wanted a new face. And now a man had appeared who was
threatening him. You are not interested in these details, are you?
Enough to say it was someone who was going to strip him of his
most valuable asset, his popularity. It was not the first time. My
client had already, by then, eliminated several rivals. That, however, was no longer sufficient. Physical elimination, I mean. The
problem had to be confronted on a more permanent basis. And his
solution was drastic and simple: it had become essential to steal
the face of the person who was preparing to replace him. In effect.
Transfer it to my client. You will agree with me that to abduct a

face is considerably less arduous than people imagine. Nobody realizes what has happened. Fascinated by the luxuriant surface, the differences that do not transcend, the ups and downs of presumed distinctions, the so-called citizens or consumers or TV viewers gulp down the same old medicine over and over in splendid new bottles. How many are there like you, who can perceive the old face repeating the old tics and tricks under the face that has recently been renovated?

At some point, however, more or less at the time when you were supposed to graduate, I was asked to a secret meeting at my client's office. He had died. A sudden death. His closest associates were shocked. An extremely dangerous vacuum of power was opening—in the enterprise, in the country, in the army, in the party, in the TV network? You do not care to go into these details, do you? It's not your cup of tea? What does matter for the understanding of our affairs is that they demanded a new transplant.

In effect. Hush up my client's demise, scrape off the pieces of his face and sew them onto the face of his younger successor, the man he himself had designated to continue his work if something happened to him. The new man would then assume his new responsibilities behind the refuge of a mask of more traditional authority. And when he had accumulated the necessary experience, his original face could then be returned to him—adjusted, naturally, in accordance with the latest polls. That is what is called fresh blood, my friend.

And that is why I was in no condition, at the time, to spend my days watching your movements and anticipating your plans. What was opening up for me was a way to intervene surgically in the lives of the most important people of our era, to institute a foundation for their permanent power, to make death or generational change but transitory destabilizers. Because if that was the first operation of the sort that I attempted, you will of course understand that it was not the last. That grayish client, whose face at least would not rest in peace, had chosen me. From that point on, it was I who started to choose which clients I would renovate, which features offered stability to the social order. So I also established, as you once did, a network: only mine is less assailable than yours.

And to this, I have dedicated my years, while you collected

useless photographs. So do not come here and threaten me with your snapshot of my hands placing minuscule devices in the basement of a face. Those clients owe everything to me. The elder ones, that they may continue to reign under the newer faces. And the young-est, that they may aspire someday to infiltrate the proudest faces of ancient power. Overlaying and undersetting, sewing on top and in between and by the side, excavating and eroding, I know who is who better than any guide that is sold in the bookstores. A snail crossing an eight-lane highway has more chances of surviving than you do. Especially if you are with that little woman. All I have to do is make a call and my friends will make sure you are suppressed, you, your photos, your former inspector, your lover's hands.

But why should I lose you again? I already made that mistake once before. I was obsessed—quite rightly—with an operation that saved the country from widespread upheaval. So I do not blame myself for disregarding your graduating ceremony—where I doubt that you received a prize. The day, I remember it as if it were yes-terday, I went to take a look at you—and you will agree that even half a look is not easy—your disappearance surprised me. Yes. As simple as that. Disappeared. It was not a matter, as it had so often been, of not being able to locate you, your face dissolving into the color of the crowd. No, this time you had really left.

You were not living with your parents, and they even became obnoxious when I sent a detective to sniff out where you had gone, as if we were reminding them of some second cousin who had died of leprosy an eternity ago and whom they preferred not to remem-ber. Something similar, though worse, happened with the neigh-bors, with your former schoolmates: the majority hardly believed you had ever existed, their eyes going blank with the effort to fix your face. They had not noticed you when you lived among them. Why should they recall you now?

The detective I hired could not catch even a scent of you. A face-less man who changes his name—because that is what you did, is it not?—is impossible to find. Particularly if he destroys all his files, all his fingerprints, any bureaucratic trail that could indicate he had ever slouched through this planet.

I was confident, nevertheless, that our paths would cross. At times, in fact, I would make some arrogant remark in the papers about my ability to operate even on someone with no countenance, to see if you might read it and come to see me on your own. It does not matter that you did not fall into that trap. You were destined to me. You do understand that, I hope? That is why you pushed your foot down on the accelerator at that intersection. Because I had been speeding through green lights for twenty years in the expectation that you would crash into me, that you would make yourself somehow manifest, if not visible. And it is better that you should have taken this long, because I am now able to offer you conditions never before possible, and for your part, weighed down as you are by that sweet woman's burden, you will have to accept what, at the time of your graduation, you might well have rejected.

You always pined for normality. Inside you there still must be someone who wants to live as the rest of us do. So what I am, in fact, suggesting is that we should revert to the first page of this book we are writing, that initial moment in which the nurse brought you to my hospital room like Moses in a basket, and I, instead of taking you in and transforming that baby into a prince, I returned you to the turbulent rivers of your life. If I am not your progenitor, I am at least a member of your family. And you have known it—fascinated by me since our crash. Otherwise, why have you been muttering your story to my absent ears all these days? Why do you come to see me, demanding favors as if I were some sort of uncle? Why should I help you if, after all calculations have been made, the only thing you have occasioned are disasters, costs without benefits, injuries to my own body?

Because you know that in me you will find a home. Maybe those extinguished eyes of yours guessed it that first day when my step-fatherly face was reflected in the remoteness of the face that you did not yet know was yours. By not intervening, I allowed you to develop your own life, which is, when you think of it, a very rich one, indeed. I used to wonder, with scientific interest, what could a child without a face make of his life? Now I know, and it seems admirable that you have defended yourself with your faculty for reading alien faces and capturing them with your camera. It could almost be said that I feel proud of you.

During that first encounter of ours in the hospital I could have committed the mistake of fixing your nose, of painting your cheeks pink, I could have reformed your features any way I wanted. The whole world would have been fascinated by you. That silly Enriqueta would have invited you not only to her birthday party but into her very conjugal bed. Everyone says that happiness cannot be bought. What can be bought, my friend, is a face. And I have got the face that you need. And I can also protect your walking-talking doll, if that is your desire, I can also give her a new face so that nobody, except for you, will recognize her.

Because it is true that she is in danger.

How can I be so sure?

A woman who was much too similar to the one you have called Patricia arrived—that same Friday that she stuck you with your defenseless playmate—at the office of a colleague of mine. It must have been Patricia because she brought with her the identical photo of your lover at four-and-a-half, the one you have handed to me. She came to ask for an urgent operation for that girl. I hope you understand, therefore, that you are not the only one who has conceived this brilliant idea. My colleague did what he always does when somebody acts suspiciously. He gave her an appointment for next week and then consulted me, as he must if he wants to retain his license to practice medicine. And since the woman was no one I knew, nor could I guess that she was someone who might interest you, I naturally authorized him to warn the police. What they do later is up to them.

You wonder about confidentiality? I am surprised that someone like you is asking that sort of question, but I'll answer it, anyway. I am scrupulous about confidentiality, thank you very much. I apply it to my habitual clientele, as well as to any person who comes well recommended. But you, of all people, cannot tell me that all the faces in the world have the same rights. If we did not relinquish, once in a while, information about some unknown, petty person, we would be breaking our pact with the authorities of this country who happen to be, as you must have realized by now, some of my best friends. Those in charge of public order respect our autonomy as doctors—as long as they know they can count on our most thorough cooperation. Or did you expect me to sacrifice my business for someone like your Alicia? Did she have anyone to protect her? Not that I knew of. Again, if I had been aware that she was a friend

of yours, if we had been partners at the time, my lips would still
be sealed. And in the case of Patricia it could even be stated that I
did you a favor: if the police had not arrested her that very Friday
afternoon, she might have pestered you to get the girl back.

But you need not worry. I don't think you'll be seeing her again.
And I am also certain that she did not let your name slip out. They
would have come to see you, wouldn't they? But beyond that elementary reasoning, I have more evidence. Yesterday a detective came
to visit this same colleague to ask him more about the girl who
appeared in the photo. They would not have frittered away their
time if they knew who was keeping her. And he also happened to
relinquish some information about your—what is it that you call
her?—your Oriana?

You have complained that nobody has ever given you friendly
advice. Let me be the first. What I think you should understand is
that women are the monarchs of deceit. I hope this paternal tone
does not disturb you, but as you have had such a paltry experience with the opposite sex, I would not want you to awaken someday with the bitter certitude that this little girl of yours had been
dissembling all this time, playing you like a saxophone until she
could find someone more powerful to guard her. Why this blind
confidence in a person you know nothing about? You said she is an
amnesiac. I would like to tell you, however, that they are searching for her because she has an excess, rather than a diminishment,
of memory. It seems that she possesses—or used to, once upon a
time, if you are correct—possesses, I say, a remarkable mnemonic
faculty. Somewhere in that mind, unbeknownst to you, she hides
what appears to be a kind of tape recorder, which reproduces with
minute faithfulness what people say. Not astonishing, is it, that
with that exceptional talent so many people want to get their hands
on her? If she were not the woman of a business associate, I myself,
let me warn you, would be making every effort I could to smuggle
my hands into that brain.

But I shall not do it. She is the one who holds you hostage for
me. If you were alone, nothing could stop you from disappearing
again, restoring your subterranean empire. The eruption into your
life of that . . . let me call her a child, of that child, has made you
visible. While you are tied to her, forget about leaving the country

or even of slipping into a multitude to snap the shot that you could sell for a fortune.

That is your real position. Take a careful look at it. Objectively. Calmly. No more network. Not a friend in the world. That soft-hearted and affectionate Jarvik, whom you compute as a last reserve, is precisely one of the men who are after your lover. And if he were to be told that you have made a fool of him, I do not think he would offer you his friendship again.

To put things clearly: without my help, there is no way in which you can save your plaything. That does not mean that I approve. But if she gives you satisfaction, if you can find in one little woman the whole world of females, all the possibilities, all the dimensions, it remains for me, as one of your principal creators, to be the best man at the wedding and to congratulate you.

You can count on me.

You can count on me. Do you know anyone else in the universe who could repeat that phrase to you?

Now you show me—silently show me—the photo you took. You do not yet let me touch it. I know what you are thinking. I may not be able to read faces as well as you, but I know what I would think in these circumstances . . . How can you trust me? What sort of guarantees can I give?

Just think a minute.

If I had wanted to capture you, would it not have been easier to blow your cover, to get one of those men who are chasing your doll to take her away, and to be left alone to excavate your skin at my leisure?

I am ready to confess that if I had believed that this plan could have been successful, I would have executed it without the slight-est hesitation. But quite frankly, my man, how do I keep you? If I put you to sleep, if I extinguish the cold semen in your eyes, your skin would stop renewing itself—you would stagnate and so would our business. There is not a jail, a hospital, an asylum, that could retain you. Of course they would begin by following my instruc-tions down to the last detail: fasten you tight, watch you day and night, surround you with reflectors as if we were about to operate. Inevitably, however, they would soon forget how dangerous you are, their attention would be distracted, and, all of a sudden, you would have escaped. And it is unpleasant to contemplate what you would do to me that night. No, my dear man, my former patient, I do not wish our little partnership to end like an action film where the hero finally, when everything seems lost, unties his bonds and wreaks a terrible revenge. No doubt gratifying to the passive, inert audience in the darkness, but not so to the one who receives the blows. Far better, wouldn't you say, to keep you happy?

Now you do pass me the photo. Without a word. Strange, to see oneself so clearly from eyes that are so alien, the lightning flash of my hands entering the mysterious waters behind that face. A memorable photo, indeed. I will try not to deny what my face is proclaiming—you have captured exactly what someone, what I myself think on those occasions. All right, I admit it, I start to think that I am possessing that face: that small apparatus is like a metallic clitoris, which I am inserting into the precise intersecting line of the brain. The photo's admonition to harbor suspicions is not misplaced.

But there is no possibility that I would do something like that to you. What function do you attribute to that piece of metal? Is it for spying? Is it a way of controlling the patient? Not at all. It is an integral part of the therapy, what we might call the postoperative treatment. Tell me: of what use is it to change somebody's twisted nose if his memory persists in remembering the old one and, therefore, continues to twist the new one until it resembles the nose that will not vanish from that memory? That is why my operations have such an incredible degree of success: because along with the old skin, they eliminate the old habits, the past. It is as if I strained my patients through a filter: like one of those that converts the dirtiest river into the most transparent drinking water. And you drink the old and purified liquid without giving a second thought to where it has been, what it has touched. My tiny device is merely guarding that new face from the ghost of the old face, making sure it cannot be recomposed. Just as we change our phone number so old lovers cannot call and make a scandal, interrupting us as we prepare to make love to our wives. But forgive that image: I forget that you would not know what I am talking about. Of course.

It is here that our interests coincide. Both of us want that sleeping beauty of a girl to stay with you, never to awaken. If that face enthuses you so, certainly, we shall make her once again into a five-year-old. And if you choose to suffocate her other faces, I will certainly not voice any opposition. But I am again appalled at your lack of ambition, my man. Why demand a dossier of her past when you can burn the memory in her? Why suffocate what you can extirpate? Irreversibly.

So she will remember only what you want her to remember.

Which does not mean that you should worry about something like that being done to you.

I would have to be insane to try to make you forget the deep pit of your previous face, that pit which has no bottom. On the contrary, what I require is that you recall it every night, that you continue to reproduce it inside over and over. My only desire is that under the faces I will settle upon you, which I have been preparing all these years, under the multiple masks, there, deep under, the cells of your original facelessness will replicate themselves like serpents during an eternity. So that each time it becomes necessary, I may descend like a miner toward the inexhaustible treasure which grows like moss on the inner wall of your most recent features.

Why should I wish to erase the incrustations that coat your skin and your memory, if your face is the only capital that you are contributing to this enterprise?

I have plans for that face.

And they are not, at this moment, the ones I dreamt of when I first saw it. Even if during all these years I have reminded myself why I should search for it. Even if up to the instant before you limped through that door I repeated that reason and no other. But now I know that we are going to postpone the distribution of those small doses of your cells among my clients, no matter how large the payments might have been. That sort of exchange will come, it will come: later.

No, my plans have changed. Your eyes have illuminated my own life as if until now I had been blind, murmuring to me that, with all my almightiness, I had been up until now a slave controlled by others, captured by their looks, relegated to exercising power through indirect, remote intermediaries. As you spoke, I managed to understand fully that thing I had glimpsed only as a weak intuition on the day I had you in these hands and dared to find in myself the courage to postpone our glory for another occasion, when you had refined the instrument of your anonymous skin and I had acquired the means to insure its use: the intuition of another future for your face.

I knew it halfway then and I know it fully at this moment and I will know it beyond any doubt within a few minutes.

I want that face for myself.

I do not know how long I will need it. A few days, a week, a year. It makes no difference. I will return it when I have tired of its exercise. I want to roam the world without anyone knowing me. I want you to open up. Open up. Open up, and let me see that which only you have seen.

Why do you look at me that way, with those forgettable eyes? With those eyes that so soon will sink into my sockets?

Let us go. If that is your desire, let us go first to undress Oriana so her memories can never more rebel. If that is your desire, if you are still doubtful, you can by yourself insert into her this apparatus, which will erase her previous faces. I shall be no more than your silent assistant, I will do no more than pass the instruments. Are you not the person who knows most about faces in the universe? Is there any other way to insure that I will not invade, with my hands, the intimate world of Oriana? Or would you prefer another sort of insurance before we operate on her? Would you prefer that before that happens we undress, you and I, underneath the lights which stream forth from the reflectors?

Here is proof of my trust.

Here is your first face.

Look at it carefully. You dimly saw it that day when the nurse brought you to the consulting room of a poor plastic surgeon. There it was, floating above your waters on the first day of your creation. Can there be more eloquent evidence of our partnership? That you should put on the only face I did not extract from nothingness, the only face that was given to me already made, that I inherited, and that now, thanks to you, I can bestow as a gift and someday recover for myself? My face.

To whom else could I offer it?

My son.

A SORT OF EPILOGUE

"Good evening, Mrs. Lynch."

"What are you doing in my house? How did you get in?"

"You are Mrs. Lynch, aren't you? Mrs. Maya Lynch?"

"But what right do you—"

"It'd be better if you sat down, madam. And please take off your raincoat. We wouldn't want your rug to get ruined."

"Though it won't be long. Just a couple of questions, ma'am, and we'll be on our way. It's about yesterday afternoon."

"But I just got back from the police. It's the third time I've had to speak to . . ."

"There are always odds and ends to clear up, Mrs. Lynch. You are Mrs. Maya Lynch, I take it?"

"I'm Maya, but no longer Mrs. Lynch. My husband and I, we've—"

"Two years ago, ma'am. We know that. But since your divorce still hasn't come through, we'll continue to call you by your married name, if you don't mind. You are, at any rate, Doctor Mavirelli's nurse. You're not denying it?"

"Why should I deny it? What I still don't know are your names."

"You do not know our names, madam, for the simple reason that we have not told them to you. Not only doctors have the privilege of confidentiality."

"Doctor Mavirelli has insisted that I see an I.D. before talking about this matter. He doesn't want journalists finding out about . . ."

"When did the doctor tell you this?"

"Yesterday."

"So you haven't seen him since the incident?"

"He gave me the rest of the week off. He asked me to cancel all his appointments."

"And he did not inform you that he was going to leave the city?"

"Has he left the city?"

"That's what we wanted to ask you, ma'am."

"I hope that you won't take this badly, but I cannot continue answering your questions until you two show me—"

"It seems you're going to have to accompany us, then, ma'am. A pity. Seeing as we've done you this big favor."

"I don't see the big favor, if you pardon me."

"No big favor? My colleague thought it would be more comfortable for you to have a little talk at your own home. The rain, and your feeling tired, things like that. But I can see he was wrong. You can admit it, man. You made a mistake, right?"

"Would you calm down, huh? The lady has never said that she wouldn't cooperate. Isn't that so, madam?"

"What are you talking about? You think I'm deaf? She's just said that she won't answer questions, thinks we're a couple of hack journalists. So you think we're journalists, Mrs. Lynch? Into the car with her. Into the car and let's get going. I'll tell you one thing, though: I'm not bringing her back. Not me. She can spend the night back there."

"Could you do me a favor? Could you help the lady with her umbrella—look at it dripping there. Where do you put your umbrella, Mrs. Lynch?"

"I can put away my own umbrella."

"You shouldn't trouble yourself. We'll take care of that. Yeah— put it in the bathroom, along with ours. Hey, you might as well take her raincoat, can you do that? She won't be needing it. That's right. Off you go . . . Let me explain, madam, just between you and me, that my colleague is not as brusque as he sounds. It so happens that he's in a hurry. He's always in a hurry, but today he has some additional reasons—let's call them of a personal nature. He has to meet someone, you understand . . . So I'm glad that we won't be forced to ask you to come along with us . . ."

"Will it take long?"

"Didn't I tell you that the man's in a hurry?"

"I don't know what else I have to add but—"

"Good. We're ready, then. And here he comes. No umbrella, no raincoat. So if you could do us the favor of sitting down. That's fine. That's the way we like it. Who's asking the questions, who's taking the notes?"

"I'll do the asking. Let's begin with that phone call to the police, ma'am. Why did you make that call?"

"I already told you people. I had the impression that the doctor—"

"You mean Doctor Mavirelli?"

"Yes, sir, that Doctor Mavirelli was in danger, that he was being threatened."

"But when the police came, you told them that it had been a false alarm, that everything was under control."

"They took quite a while to come, sir, a good half-hour."

"A good half-hour? Are you sure about that?"

"Yes, sir. I was surprised, too. I hope you won't take this badly, but the services are steadily getting worse in this city."

"So that so much time had passed that you thought everything was all right?"

"That's what I thought, sir. You couldn't hear a thing from the doctor's private operating room, so I thought that—"

"And were you surprised when the police insisted on seeing the doctor and found the patient dead?"

"I wouldn't call him a patient, sir, if you'll allow me, because the truth is that it was the woman who had come for the operation."

"He wasn't a patient? How can you be so sure? Were you with them during the . . . let's see, almost two hours they were inside?"

"Of course not. I was outside. But there's no plastic surgeon like Doctor Mavirelli in the country. Maybe in the world. There was time for an operation, I'll admit that. Because what the papers say, sir, that's the holy truth. In fifteen minutes, at times twenty, he can alter a face so that you—"

"It's clear you're loyal to your employer, madam. We like that."

"Yeah, we really like to see loyalty in times like these, ma'am, but we don't need you to sell us the merchandise, you know. We

124

understand the doctor's famous. But I don't intend to have an operation, so you can spare me the propaganda."

"It's not propaganda, sir. I was saying it because if the doctor had operated on that man, I can assure you that some improvement of his face would have been noticeable. He would have made it at least a bit more . . . well, flashy. Showy. And this man, the holy truth is that I had never seen a less important face. To the point that when he came yesterday after lunch, I almost didn't let him in. The doctor had canceled all his appointments, so I thought it would be somebody more—well, at any rate, not a man so, I don't know, common. He was Mr. Nobody. Not like the doctor's usual clients."

"And how do you explain, then, that they spent so much time, both of them, inside Doctor Mavirelli's operating room?"

"You'd have to ask the doctor that."

"We've already asked him, ma'am. He invokes his right to confidentiality, won't comment on the matter. And today we haven't even been able to find him. That's why we'd like to know your version of the whole thing."

"The doctor was worried by a car crash he had been in, Christmas Eve it was. I don't know the details, but he was awfully glad when that man called up and asked to see him. It seems he was ready to take the blame if the doctor did a favor for the man's girl friend."

"And that wasn't unusual, that sort of swap?"

"The doctor says that you don't always have to demand payment in money. He says that people have a lot of other services to offer. And if they took their time, it must have been because the man was the jealous type, maybe he wanted to know each particular of the operation."

"But the doctor never operated on the girl."

"The girl?"

"The girl, ma'am, the woman who was to be operated on, the woman with the bandaged face."

"Oh, you mean the woman. She didn't move an inch, during those two hours, from the window. The only thing she asked me was if there was an emergency exit. I told her yes. Even added that this business couldn't be run without an emergency exit, hoping that maybe she'd answer and that way we could pass the time with a little talk, but she didn't say another word and I left her alone. I'm used to being absolutely discreet."

"So you don't know the names of Doctor Mavirelli's clients."

"No, and if I did, I wouldn't give them to you. But I do happen to know that they are influential people. Very influential. The doctor has always told me that if I ever need any—"

"And she did not move from the window during the whole time?"

"No, sir."

"So the doctor could not have had occasion to change her face?"

"I already told you it could not have happened."

"And you never saw her face? The doctor never saw it?"

"No, sir. I already told you that—look, quite frankly, I do not see that I am adding anything new to the deposition I already gave yesterday and this morning and now, this afternoon."

"What if you let me decide what matters and what doesn't, huh, lady?"

"You'll have to pardon my colleague's brusqueness, madam, but what he's saying is true. You call the shots in the doctor's consulting room, we call the shots in what we ask here. Just keep on telling the story."

"All of a sudden the bandaged woman stood up. She had seen something through the window—or so it seemed."

"You saw what she had seen?"

"No, sir, I was behind the desk."

"How do you know what she saw, then?"

"I don't know, sir. I only know that it was something that struck . . . terror in her heart. Yes. She was terrorized."

"And it had to be something she saw through the window."

"I don't know what else it could have been. She was looking at the street without a peep for two hours. Suddenly she gets up and tells me that they're coming."

"They? You're sure?"

"She said they, sir. So it must have been more than one man, at least two. She rushed to the emergency exit, and I—well, I was really astonished, but I managed to ask her if she wanted to leave a message for the doctor or the gentleman—I called him that, though

the truth is that I don't think he was any gentleman at all—if she
wanted to leave some sort of message. And she answered, 'He won't
be needing me, anymore.'"

"That he wouldn't be needing her, anymore? Which of the
two?"

"I beg your pardon, sir?"

"Which of the two, the doctor or her friend—which one was
she leaving the message for?"

"Which of the two? The truth is that I didn't think to ask that
question. I supposed it was for her friend. She didn't even know
the doctor."

"And she took off the bandage?"

"No, sir. Though in the street she must have, because otherwise
she would have attracted everybody's attention. You can't go far
with a bandage like that on, sir."

"And you haven't seen her since then, ma'am?"

"No, sir. Why should I see her? Has she done anything
wrong?"

"What she's done or not done is not a matter that should concern
you. What we're interested in is why you called the police."

"I'll tell you, sir. When the doctor came out with that man and
they didn't find the woman, the truth is that—the man turned
violent. Agitated, I believe that's the word I used originally, but I
wouldn't be wrong to call it violence. He ran to the window to see
if the woman—"

"Ran?"

"Yes, sir, he went running."

"Not limping?"

"The one who was limping, it seems to me, was the doctor. Due
to the accident. But I may be confused."

"You may well be. And so the man . . ."

"I was alarmed, sir. I thought he was going to throw himself out
the window. And then he turned, and without a word he looked at
the doctor as if asking him where the woman was, as if the doctor
had stolen her. I felt scared."

"And why were you so scared?"

"Because of the eyes, sir. They were, I don't know, sir—it's as if
they were dead, sir."

"Dead? Did you say dead?"

"Yes, sir."

"And you read a lot of horror novels, huh, lady?"

"I would ask you, sir, that you keep to yourself any snide comments you may have. If you're interested in continuing this conversation . . ."

"And through all of this, the doctor . . ."

"He was pale. Breathing with his mouth closed. I know that he says that the whole affair did not affect him at all and that it is quite normal in his sort of work that people should just up and go, disappear before an operation. But in spite of what he says, he seemed very—dismayed, I would say. Beside himself, almost. Calm, though. As if some tragedy had fallen upon him, the funeral of someone dearly beloved."

"And that's why you called the police?"

"No, sir, not yet. He stayed there—"

"The doctor?"

"Yes, sir. The doctor stayed there as if rooted to the floor, watching that man striding up and down, up and down, and then, all of a sudden, as if he were wakening from a nightmare—"

"Definitely too many novels, ma'am."

"You heard what Mrs. Lynch said. Those sort of remarks bother her."

"But she should know that I'm not to blame. Yes, ma'am, it's not me who's saying this about you. It's the doctor himself. He's the one who says that you're exaggerating all the time, that your only defect is an excess of imagination."

"The doctor said that? About me? I have never in my whole life heard him make any comment of the sort about me or about any—"

"We've heard all this before. What you still haven't been able to explain, ma'am, is why you called the police."

"Well, this man began to act unpleasant. The doctor suggested they go talk inside and the man didn't want to, and then he said something about there being nothing more to talk about."

"And what do you think he was referring to?"

"I thought that since the doctor hadn't been able to operate on his girl friend, the man was no longer willing to take the blame for the accident. At any rate, they finally went in and then . . . well, inside, the doctor, or the other one, bumped into some test tubes and they fell and I heard the noise and I thought there was a fight going on and that the Doctor was in danger, and then, I know it was silly of me, but I called the police."

"Without asking your employer's permission?"

"I was scared, sir."

"And you don't think that there could indeed have been a fight and that your employer killed that patient?"

"How could I possibly think such a thing? He died of cardiac arrest. When we went in, he had just expired. The doctor was trying to revive him. There he was, crouched over the body, trying to return it to life. It made me afraid at first, because it was as if his hands were coming out of the dead body, as if they were coming from deep inside. It took him a good while to lift his eyes. And he was very distressed."

"Crying?"

"I couldn't say, sir. Distressed."

"And why did you declare, the first time, that he had something strange in his eyes? That he had, that his eyes were . . . burned out, you said."

"That was a mistake on my part, sir. I was talking about the other one, the dead man."

"We rather doubt it, ma'am. You were talking about the doctor. 'He was—unrecognizable.' That's what you said at your first interrogation. 'It made me afraid, that's the holy truth. When I saw his eyes. It was as if they were burned out, the color of ashes.'"

"That's impossible, sir. Doctor Mavirelli—look, if I had to describe the doctor's eyes, I'd describe them more like burning coals. Full of fire, of life."

"But your first impression was not quite that, was it?"

"I didn't look much at him, sir, if you want to know the truth. I was more interested in the fact that the dead man was smiling."

"Go on. Why are you stopping now?"

"You're going to make fun of me again."

"Madam, I can promise you that my colleague will not make fun of you because of anything that you say."

"He'll say I have too much imagination and that I read too many novels, that's what he's going to say."

"A promise is a promise, madam. Tell us about the smile."

"You can see it for yourselves. You have the body, don't you?"

"No, ma'am, we don't have the body."

"It was returned to Doctor Mavirelli, Mrs. Lynch."

"It was returned to him? I thought that first an autopsy had to be performed."

"The doctor called up a couple of his friends and orders came from above that the body was to be turned over to him. He said he was in a hurry. That there are certain delicate tissues that can be ruined in an autopsy and that this was a case of great scientific interest and . . . well, you can understand that we were surprised. Because we weren't aware that doctors have now become the owners of each patient who dies in their operating room, nobody had told us that was the law."

"But somebody must have come forward to claim the body."

"You want to know something, Mrs. Lynch? Between you and us? You want to know? Nobody came forward for that body. No family, no friends, nobody. Because we don't even know who the man is. The slightest notion. There's not a reference in the files, not a photograph, not a clue."

"But Doctor Mavirelli must have some idea."

"A false name, madam. He's an N.N. As anonymous as any of the drunkards who die on the street. More anonymous."

"What I don't understand is that a person like that—I mean, he couldn't have had a very gratifying existence, sir, if you see what I mean . . . how he could smile like that. I had never seen a smile like that one, sir. So serene, so peaceful. An unforgettable face, sir. Because of the smile. It's—it's enough to make you feel envious, you know. If you could have seen it."

"If we could have seen it? If we could have seen it?"

"What my colleague is trying to explain is that we have seen any number of smiles like that one. Over and over and over again. Even in our dreams, madam, we see those smiles."

"But we'd rather not speak about that smile, Mrs. Lynch. It's a fucking smile, lady, if you pardon my language. At first it obsessed

me, of course it did. Just like it does you. Then I said to myself, if
these poor assholes want to die happy, what do I care? And I began
to treat that smile as if it were a member of the family who's dying
and whom no one wants to talk about. Like a fart that someone
lets loose in a cathedral and that no one wants to notice. If you
pardon my language."

"So let's not refer to that smile, anymore, madam, not one more
word, if you don't mind. There's in fact something else we're interested in, if you want to know the truth . . ."

"Yes, ma'am. Those eyes you mentioned . . ."

"Those eyes? The dead man's eyes?"

"The dead man's eyes? Well, if that's what you want. Certainly,
ma'am. Let's talk about those eyes, if those are the ones you'd like
to talk about."

"In effect, Mrs. Lynch. What color did you say they were?"

TO BE CONTINUED

Afterword

Mascara, first published in Spanish (in Argentina) and English in 1988, is a challenging, intricately constructed novel. Its time scheme is particularly complex, even labyrinthine. The most useful first step a commentator can undertake is to lay out in simple form the story material that Ariel Dorfman has worked with.

One day, in a year that we can perhaps pin down as 1973, a house in a city that may be Santiago, Chile, is raided by police agents who in the course of their depredations do something to a four-year-old child, Oriana, that amounts to rape. As a result she appears to suffer an arrest in her mental growth: she remains frozen in childhood, even though her body continues to grow normally.

In fact Oriana has undergone a split. Henceforth she will have two selves; more and more sternly the arrested child self will deny the developing self access to their joint physical body.

The growing self goes out among the despised and rejected of her country, hears their stories—the stories, as she puts it, of their hands—and stores them up in her memory for some longed-for future. If she could only find a community of like minds, she thinks, she could begin the salvation of the country. But she is alone; the stories are doomed to die with her.

The last time this growing self is allowed to see the world through physical eyes is when, on the street, men advance toward her to arrest her for her activities. Thereafter the body the two had shared is taken over entirely by the child self.

There is a gap in time. The next we know, a woman named Patricia brings Oriana to what is meant to be a safe house.

The safe house belongs to a strange being, a man who was born faceless and is therefore, as he puts it, "semi-invisible." His

---

J. M. COETZEE, who won the Nobel Prize for Literature in 2003, is the author of eight novels. He lives in Australia, where he is a research fellow at the University of Adelaide.

facelessness is not a physical deformity such as we find in medical textbooks. It is rather a nullity, an absence of feature. Photographed, he leaves no trace on the film. If we as readers have trouble in visualizing such a being, that is because his face cannot be represented. It is beyond the reach of language.

The faceless man, who is never named, suffered a miserable childhood. His parents were successful members of the middle class. His father sold surgical instruments that allow doctors to explore the interiors of bodies; his mother was a makeup artist who created faces for the media. They neglected him; most of the time they did not even register his presence.

As a child he developed a passion for photography, in which he found erotic pleasure. In fact, while "normal" sex filled him with revulsion, taking a picture brought him to orgasm.

Ignored on all sides, the faceless man has in the course of time been taken over by a spirit of vengefulness. He has given up his vain longing to be seen, to become part of the social world. Instead he embraces his own invisibility and the power it gives him. Like Shakespeare's Iago, he in effect says, "Evil, be thou my good."

At the time when Oriana comes into his life, he is working as an archivist in the Department of Traffic Accidents, where he uses his superhuman memory for faces, a collection of compromising photographs he has taken, and threats of blackmail, to create a clandestine network of power.

Oriana is not the first woman the faceless man has known. Two years ago there had been Alicia, with whom he had spent a brief, happy week. Alicia, an ugly person herself, had brought him back to humanity by looking at him and recognizing him. But Alicia, a member of the political underground, had been betrayed to the police by a plastic surgeon who had worked on her, Dr. Miravelli. For this act the faceless man has marked Miravelli down for retribution.

Now Patricia, an old associate of Alicia's, brings Oriana to the faceless man's home. The net is closing: in a few days Patricia herself will be hunted down by the state and murdered.

Unlike adults, Oriana has not constructed a face for herself. She is the only person the faceless man has met who is her true self. During her stay with him, he learns that she lives entirely in the present. Each day the previous day is wiped from her memory. Thus her life is a perpetual adventure of discovery.

He has no identity, she has no past. They are like twins. In her company he feels he is becoming young again.

But there is a threat to his happiness. What if the mature Oriana returns to take over the body he loves? What if this menacing self is lurking nearby, or lies beside them in their bed while they make love, biding her time?

In order to locate and destroy the adult Oriana, the faceless man seeks for a photograph of her in the archives of the state. But Miravelli is a step ahead of him. Miravelli has penetrated and taken over his network, and cut off his access to the archives.

Using his last resources, the faceless man purloins the photograph of Oriana in Miravelli's own files. It is useless to him: it shows a child of four.

Who is Miravelli?

Dr. Miravelli has made his fortune creating faces for the rich. His powers are almost magical. When his most famous patient dies, for instance, he is able to transfer his face to the body of a younger man and thus prolong this politician's career indefinitely.

Miravelli came across the faceless man as a baby, and realized at once that through him he could attain limitless power. He wants to use the faceless man as a source of skin cells which can then be fused to other surfaces, making them invisible.

Using his own powers, the faceless man has thus far evaded Miravelli. But now a fateful event occurs. The faceless man and Miravelli come together in a traffic accident, and the faceless man—rashly, as it turns out—determines to sue Miravelli and use the publicity of the courts to expose him.

With the aid of an Oriana swathed in bandages, he has gained access to Miravelli's surgery, copied Miravelli's patient lists, and photographed a vampire-like Miravelli performing an operation during which he implants a mysterious little device inside the reconstructed face of his patient.

He threatens to publish this photograph unless Miravelli implants one of his devices in Oriana, freezing her for ever in her child state.

Miravelli, whose secret plan is to take over the faceless man's face and become invisible himself, agrees to meet him. Shortly before their rendezvous, the faceless man writes what turn out to be his last words, the history that forms the first part of *Mascara*.

Of what happens at the meeting we learn only indirectly, from the interrogation of Miravelli's secretary by two state operatives that constitutes the Epilogue. The faceless man has died on Miravelli's operating table, but appeared to die with a smile on his face (and therefore with a face). His body has disappeared, whisked away by Miravelli's underlings.

MASCARA IS SET in a police state of a Chilean or Argentine variety, replete with a thuggish secret police, networks of informers, unexplained deaths and disappearances, and a slavish media.

It is clear from even a summary of the novel that its characters come from popular genres: the horror story, the thriller, the fantasy romance. Dorfman has been a pioneer, in Latin America, in the deconstruction of imported popular culture, in particular the mythic stories that originate in the culture factories of the USA. His widely influential *How to Read Donald Duck* was first published in Chile in 1971.

One of the targets of *Mascara* is the intrinsic superficiality of a political culture based on television images. In such a culture, a creator and manager of images like Dr. Miravelli becomes the power behind the throne.

But Dorfman's analysis of the superficies goes further (one hesitates to say "deeper") than this. In the shifting area between the real and the fantastic in which the action of *Mascara* takes place, the face is no longer part of our natural self but belongs instead to culture. The face is a mask that we inherit, largely from our parents. The son inherits and renews his father's face/mask. Thus is the patriarchal order perpetuated.

Our face is part of our self-presentation, like our clothes, but we cannot take it off as we take off our clothes. Yet it is an error to think that beneath the face we wear is our true self, for there is no such thing as not wearing a face. One exception to this rule is a young child whose face has not yet set, particularly a young girl child like Oriana. Another is the faceless man. But neither a young child nor a faceless man can participate in the social order.

Not only is the face we had thought part of our natural self now, in *Mascara*, detached from nature and reallocated to culture. Our hands too are not part of our natural selves, as we see in the second part of the book, the part devoted to Oriana. What we think of as our hands are shells; they conceal secret hands with a life of their own.

In the fantastic and sometimes surreal world of *Mascara*, which mirrors the surreal underlife of the modern world we have created for ourselves, the organs of pleasure are in the process of migrating from the genitals to the eyes and brain. Both the faceless man, sent into orgasmic transports by photographs, and Miravelli, gloating over the bodies of insensible patients, exemplify the shift toward scopophilia.

One of the notable aspects of *Mascara* is thus its exploration of the metamorphoses of power, political and sexual and political-sexual, an exploration which looks toward William Burroughs in one direction and Jacques Lacan in another. *Mascara* puts in question such natural-seeming distinctions as between exterior and interior, appearance and truth, image and reality.

Like such monsters as Dr. Frankenstein's creature and the hunchback of Notre Dame, the faceless man is a figure of both horror and pathos. He longs to be loved, but more fundamentally he longs to be seen: "We require someone to look at us in order to exist," he says. He dies at Miravelli's hands, but the comic-book ending seems to promise a resurrection: "TO BE CONTINUED."

Mascara is the fourth novel in the oeuvre of a bilingual writer who has contributed to both the Hispanic and the English-language literature of our times. Born in Argentina of Jewish immigrant parents, Ariel Dorfman spent some of his childhood and youth in the United States, some in Chile, his successive migrations dictated by successive waves of right-wing repression. His career as a writer had barely begun when he was forced into exile by the Pinochet coup: his first novel, the (revised) English version of which is known as *Hard Rain*, appeared in 1973. The next three novels were written in exile: *Widows* (Mexico City, 1981, revised

1985), *The Last Song of Manuel Sendero* (Mexico City, 1982, revised 1989), and *Mascara* (Buenos Aires, 1988). Notable works since *Mascara* include the play *Death and the Maiden*, first performed in 1990, the novels *Konfidenz* (1994) and *The Nanny and the Iceberg* (1999), and the memoir *Heading South, Looking North* (1998).

J. M. Coetzee

About the Author

ARIEL DORFMAN has been hailed by the *Washington Post* as a "world novelist of the first order" and by *Newsweek* as "one of the greatest Latin American novelists." A Chilean expatriate, now professor at Duke University, Dorfman has seen his works translated into more than thirty languages and his plays performed in over one hundred countries. His play *Death and the Maiden* was made into a film by Roman Polanski. His most recent books are *Exorcising Terror: The Incredible Unending Trial of General Augusto Pinochet* (Seven Stories Press, 2003) and *Desert Memories: Journeys Through the Chilean North* (National Geographic Books, 2004). His novels *Widows*, *Konfidenz*, and *The Nanny and the Iceberg* have just been reissued. Two of Dorfman's new plays will appear in 2005, *The Other Side* in London's West End, and *Purgatorio* on Broadway. He lives with his wife, Angélica, in Durham, North Carolina.